The Rainbow's Dark Shadow
a novel by

Sharon E. Cargo

The Rainbow's Dark Shadow
Cover Design by Ashley Brown

For information on ordering please contact:
Vision Publishing
1115 D Street, Ramona, CA 92065
760-789-4700
www.visionpublishingservices.com
Printed in the United States of America

Dedication

Dedicated to the memory of Dr. Henry Morris

whose careful scientific and theological research

made this work possible

Acknowledgements

I would like to especially recognize the contributions to this novel by the Ramona Christian Writers Critique group. The encouragement and input of Jim Wray, Pam Orlina, Peter Zindler, Adelaide Zindler, Gail Prout, Suzanne Middlebrooks, Byron Mettler, and Edna Hill were invaluable during the writing of *The Rainbow's Dark Shadow*. Peter Zindler, an associate minister at Bayview Baptist Church and Dr. Gary Bassham, senior pastor of Mountain View Community Church, contributed greatly to the theology of this work. However, any theological mistakes or Biblical misconceptions are entirely my fault.

I would like to thank the staff of the Institute for Creation Research. They contributed to my education as a student at ICR and their influence has continued, as I became an Instructor there. Their research and publications have changed many lives. They are on the frontlines of the battlefield of compromise. This book is dedicated to the memory of Dr. Henry Morris, the founder of ICR and the "father of modern creationism".

I would like to thank my family: my husband, Bob, for his support, both technical and emotional and my sister Theresa for the final editing. I would like to thank my children Brian, Erin and Kevin, who brought untold joy into my life and for growing up and being self-sufficient enough to give me time to write.

Daniel Romero of Vision Publishing was invaluable in the preparation and publishing of the manuscript.

Introduction

We know very little about the pre-Flood world. The Bible tells us it was so violent that God repented of creating man. We are also told that Noah was the only righteous man on earth after the death of Methuselah. The Bible further explains that Noah's family was saved with him, but tells us very little of their characters. The establishment of a wicked society and pagan religion occurred almost as soon as the Ark landed. Dr. Henry Morris believed that very possibly one of the Ark residents brought the rudiments of the pre-Flood religion with them and secretly practiced it until there were enough followers to practice it openly. He also thought it likely that Satan was in direct communication with those in rebellion against God. These two concepts are the basis of this novel.

We are also told that the end times will be similar to the "days of Noah", or the immediate pre-Flood world. If we are close to the end times, as many believe, then the pre-Flood world reflects our own society. The practice of widespread drug use is not new to the modern world; botanical products have been used throughout history for medicinal, religious and recreational purposes. The violence produced when drug distribution becomes an economic issue is all too apparent in our own times and no doubt was part of the violence of the pre-Flood life.

The Nephilim, a breed of giants whose origin is explained as a result of the "sons of God taking wives from the daughters of men" typified the violence of the times. Although their existence is explained, the definition of the 'sons of God' and the 'daughters of men', the Bible leaves open for interpretation. Some believe the sons of God were the descendents of Seth and the daughters of men were the descendents of Cain. This seems unlikely because traditionally, (not necessarily Biblically), Noah's wife was a Cain descendent and Noah a Seth descendant. God blessed their union. In any case, the Nephilim were large, violent and evil.

The long ages attained by pre-Flood humans are well documented in the Bible. Since these individuals lived hundreds of years, their physical development was very likely at a slower pace than our physical development is today. The onset of puberty was likely well into their twenties or even beyond. Thus, Noah's three sons did not marry or have children until they were close to one hundred years old. *In the Rainbow's*

Dark Shadow, the fictional character, Cassie, at eighteen is just reaching puberty and relatively un-prepared for motherhood.

On the other hand, Dr. Morris pointed out that it would be rather unusual for Noah to wait until he was five hundred to marry and have children. This is not to say that it didn't happen that way, but leads us to two interesting possibilities: 1) Noah may have been married to someone else before he married the woman with whom he fathered Shem, Ham, and Japheth, and/or 2) there were possibly other children who chose not to accept the safety of the Ark. This novel explores both of these possibilities.

Some may wonder why I chose to use modern English. We don't know what language was used prior to the Tower of Babel, but it was probably very close to Hebrew and it was certainly not formal King James English. The characters are a family living and working closely together; therefore I chose a rather casual tone for the conversations. Not only does an informal tone seem likely, but also is more enjoyable to the reader. I don't know Hebrew, so the language is English

Although I made every attempt to make this work compatible with a literal, young-earth interpretation of the Biblical account in Genesis, do not take it too seriously. Don't bother to look up the names of Noah's wife and daughters–in–law, they are unknown. This book is what it is - a novel, a work of fiction meant for entertainment. Please relax and enjoy the story.

Chapter 1

Tymorrah, Sunday, December 7, 2349 BC

Emzara froze. Terrified, she dropped her basket of vegetables. Tomatoes, peppers and squash rolled unnoticed at her feet. The meaning of that drop of water on her face was clear and nothing else mattered, not now, not ever again. She had lived with Noah long enough to know that drop meant her crazy ex-husband was right. It meant they were all going to die. She ran screaming into the house. It was empty except for her husband.

"Jovan!"

"Jovan!" She found him in his workshop, carving one of the gods they sold to a supplier in the city.

"Hurry! We have to leave! Water is falling from the sky! We have to find Noah!"

"What? Are you insane? Noah would not help us, even if we found him, remember you are his ex-wife and I was once his friend."

"Yes, yes he would! You know he's not like that. He would do anything to help anybody."

"Emzara, you're as crazy as he is. Go ahead and go. I'm sure you will be back as soon as you realize your hysteria is groundless. Water has never fallen from the sky and it never will. There isn't enough water on earth to cover the entire world. Noah's nuts. I'll stay here and take my chances; nothing is going to happen. Anyway, I couldn't face Noah after all these years, not for any reason. How could I? I'm never going to admit to him that he's right, even if by some weird circumstance he appears to be."

"Jovan, you don't understand! Water is falling from the sky. Soon there will be no dry land to escape to. We have to go. Now!"

He turned his back and returned to his carving, "You go. Satisfy your curiosity. When you get back, never mention Noah to me again. I am tired of hearing about him."

The raindrops were falling harder now. Emzara abandoned her plans of packing anything and ran to the stable. An atmosphere of confusion and fear filled the barnyard: birds flying in every direction, dogs howling, cows stomped and uneasily called to their calves. The horses were spooked. The normally calm team that pulled their cart was running around the paddock wildly. They were terrified of the beads of water that relentlessly fell on their backs. Just as Emzara approached, one of the horses blindly hit the wooden fence. The fence broke with a loud crack; pieces of wood flew into the air while the impact sent the mare to her knees. She struggled to her feet bleeding from several large splinters protruding from her neck and withers. She shuddered violently throwing blood and debris over the small enclosure.

As if of one mind both horses quickly escaped through the break in the fence. They galloped down the grassy slope kicking their heals in their search for shelter from the drops of water that were falling harder as every minute passed. The injured horse slipped on the wet grass and tumbled down the hill. Her back legs flipped over her head and Emzara heard a loud snap as the horse's neck broke. The mare's body shook momentarily before she died. Her teammate never looked back.

Emzara had no choice but to try to reach the Ark on foot. It was only a few miles; surely she could make it in time. She had no doubt Noah would let her in. *I know he still loves me. Why did I ever leave him? Why didn't I go back?* She knew why. Life with Noah was embarrassing, everyone jeering and calling him crazy. She couldn't stand it anymore. She was running now and her thoughts were running as well. But the embarrassment wasn't the only reason; Noah had become boring. Jovan offered excitement and a carefree, indulgent life for her and her children. *My children! I have doomed my children! They should rightfully be on the Ark now with their father and I led them astray.* She used their feelings of rebellion against the restraints of their rigid upbringing to turn them all against Noah. Emzara convinced Noah's children he was crazy and even dangerous. And who could blame her? Everyone thought he was crazy. Gods don't talk to people. Sane people don't build giant boats on dry land and rant about the end of the world.

Where am I anyway? It was difficult to see through the sheets of water. She could only hope that at least some of her children and their families made it to the Ark. The grass was slippery and she fell several times. *Maybe I'll be lucky and break my neck like that poor horse.* Drenched and muddy she made it to the top of the hill where she had been able to see the Ark's construction. Even that distant view embarrassed her. Now she understood his obsession, racing to build his boat before God's promised destruction. *I loved him so! Why didn't I believe him? What is that noise?* Through the din of the storm she could hear an eerie clamor. *What is that?* With a sinking heart she realized the noise was the combined voices of thousands of people wailing and pleading to be let on the Ark. She raced down the hill into the knee-high water. *Surely Noah would let her in, but how was she going to let him know she was here? How was she going to get through this hysterical crowd, each of them realizing that they and their children were about to die?*

Those close enough to beat upon the Ark did so, their hands bleeding from the repeated impact. All screamed and pleaded for admittance. Some desperately; tried to defy gravity by climbing the slanted and pitched hull of the boat, only to fall flaying back into the water from the slippery planks.

Then someone recognized her. "Hey! That's his first wife! Maybe he'll open the door for her!"

A large man lifted her onto his shoulders, "Call to him, when he opens the ramp, we'll rush in."

"Noah! Noah! It's me. Zara. Please let us in. I believe you now! You know I always loved you. Please."

Emzara did as she was told, even though she knew it wouldn't work. Noah could never hear her, and if he did open the Ark, the water would gush in and all these people and the now waist high water would surely sink it. The throng of people along with terrified and bleating animals swam desperately but Emzara noticed their numbers were steadily decreasing, as their desperation did nothing to prevent them from becoming victims of the raging Flood.

"Noah! Please! Do you want me to die?"

"I can't hold you any longer. He's not opening the ramp! I'm going to run for higher ground."

Before he could put her down, a wave of water drove several people into them. He kept his balance for a few seconds and then they both fell into the rising floodwaters. It seemed like a thousand feet kicked her. Her own legs were so tangled in her saturated clothes that she couldn't move at all. Exhausted, she stopped struggling. Death was inevitable now. She wondered if Noah would remember her in his new life. With one more gust of energy, she tried reflexively to reach the surface.

***

Emzara awoke to sunlight streaming into her bedroom. Relief flooded over her. *It was just a dream, terrifying but only a dream. Maybe it was a vision sent from God to warn me, to tell me that Noah isn't crazy and that the Flood he keeps raving about will become a reality. Thank goodness, I was just about to leave him. I need to break things off with Jovan.*

She sighed. Flirting with Jovan was fun and exhilarating. Hiding their relationship from Noah wasn't all that difficult, since Noah was so preoccupied. He spent all of his time building that ridiculous boat. But she didn't really love Jovan; at least not the way she loved Noah. She looked down at Noah's hand, draped across her waist. So strong and his body was so warm and comforting next to hers. *No, I will never leave him. I will just have to learn to deal with all the embarrassment, the jeering and mocking. The children and I will just stay home.*

She could hear her children outside laughing and playing. *I suppose that I really should get up and make their breakfast. Hmm...what to make. Pocket bread sandwiches, filled with tomatoes, onions and green leafy lettuce, all fresh from the garden, and still warm from the sun. I'll drizzle just a little herb, oil and vinegar dressing over the filling. Maybe I'll put in some cheese. No, some of the kids don't like cheese. I'll just slice some and put it on the table. I'll have the older kids pick some peaches. We can peal and slice them and eat them with some fresh cream.* She was making herself hungry.

Emzara put her hand on Noah's to move it so she could get up. She quickly dropped it. Something very strange was happening. Noah's skin was turning to rough, brittle scales. His nails were growing longer and curling, becoming claws right before her eyes. She turned to find the man in her bed was a hideous beast, laughing at her terror.

The bed disappeared; she was lying on cold, slimy rocks. The sunlight turned to dim reflected firelight. The air was unbearable. It was hot and a putrid smell burned her nostrils. Her children's laughter had turned into wails. They were begging for something. *What, what was it they were saying so desperately?* Now she could hear splashing, and pleas for their father to let them on the Ark. They were adults now and carried their children and grandchildren above their heads, giving them a few more moments of life. Then silence. They all drowned.

Thus began Emzara's sojourn in the afterlife, forced to view a never-ending parade of the detailed deaths of her children, grandchildren and great-grandchildren. As they were dying she was painfully aware they all blamed her. Sometimes, as a 'special treat' she was allowed to see the deaths of all those she had directly or indirectly influenced to reject Noah's preaching. The phrase "why should we believe him if his own wife doesn't even believe him" was repeated constantly. During her lifetime, in the brief moments she had contemplated death and the afterlife, she had imagined an everlasting peace, an eternal comfort and release from earthly duties. Here there was no peace, no refuge and no comfort. There was only a continuous repetition after repetition of the Flood, her deceptive awakening in Noah's bed, followed by the reality of Hell and constant remorse.

Chapter 2

The Ark, 2348 BC

Debra threw her hands to her mouth to stifle a scream of horror. There was no doubt in her mind what her sister-in-law was doing. Debra had been present at this type of ceremony many times in the city, before the deluge, before she met Shem.

Just a few moments ago, she was awakened by what sounded like a baby's cry. Then it suddenly stopped. She was sure it couldn't really be a baby, there were only eight of them on board, and they were all adults. *Maybe one of the lambs or kids is out of its pen. I better get up and investigate.* As she stepped outside of her room, Debra was immediately drawn to a flickering of candlelight coming from the partially ajar door of a small storage room, across from the living quarters. *Was someone else awake? Maybe they needed her help*, after all the sound that awakened her had come from that direction. Besides, she was just plain curious.

She wished she had ignored her curiosity rather than view this scene. Her sister-in-law, Zalith, was holding a lifeless infant before an image. From her angle, she couldn't see the statue well, but she really didn't need to see it. She knew such sacrifices were made to Inanna, the patron goddess of the city, Tymorrah, where she had lived before she married Shem.

The child Zalith held looked like a newborn, but small, probably premature. *But where did it come from? Was it Zalith's?* She knew the priestesses at the temple possessed special herbs; medications to induce early labor, and sacrifices of such premature infants had been common. *Did Zalith bring those herbs with her? Just in case?*

This had to be Zalith's own child. *No wonder she started wearing the long loose robes like the rest of us!* Her father-in-law, Noah, had asked, or rather commanded, that his three sons and their wives refrain from procreative sexual activity until the waters retreated from the earth. He didn't think the Ark was a good place to raise children; children needed sunshine and room to run. Besides everyone was so busy caring for the animals, there wasn't much time to dedicate to child rearing.

Was this Zalith's reasoning, to kill her own child to prevent detection of a forbidden pregnancy? Possibly, but Debra knew that her in-laws would welcome and nurture a grandchild, especially since the rain had finally stopped, and especially if the child was Ham and Zalith's. They were the favored ones, the beautiful ones. Debra couldn't really blame Noah and Naamah for their favoritism. Ham and Zalith were such a beautiful contrast. The combination of her radiant features, fair skin, blond wavy hair and blue eyes with his handsome face, dark skin, dark eyes, and curly hair would surely make beautiful children. And they seemed so much in love: always off by themselves laughing at some secret joke between them. She had thought they would be doting parents. *But wait, did Ham know about the baby? He must!*

She would worry about that later. Now she needed someplace to hide. Zalith was coming out of her trance, wrapping the body of the infant, cleaning up the blood, and putting her candles and goddess into a heavy fabric bag. Debra quickly dove into another storage room, where she hoped she would be undetected. She hid in the shadows as Zalith walked past. She was wearing the long robe and cone shaped hat of a Temple Priestess, richly embroidered with symbols of what Shem called the 'heathen astrology'. She shuddered when she heard the splash as Zalith threw the body overboard.

Zalith disappeared into the hallway that led to her room. Debra lay curled up in shock, her cries no longer repressed as sobs racked her body. How could God have allowed this? Wasn't this the reason the rest of the world had been destroyed? Her friends, sisters, and even her parents had died for committing such crimes.

She still had nightmares about the day the Ark was lifted off the ground by the surging flood waters, hearing again the desperate cries outside the Ark as the others realized that Noah was right. She was sure she heard her name called out in desperation, her family begging her to open the door. If she could have, she would have opened the ramp and let them in. But God had miraculously sealed it. Shem had tried to comfort her that night alone in their warm bed.

"Honey, it's not your fault. Remember, we tried to warn them. They could all be safe with us now. It was their choice. And anyway, who are we to question God?"

"Shem, that's easy for you to say when your family is safe. I heard mine drowning and pleading for me to save them! What if they had a last minute change of heart; would God save their souls from eternal torture?"

"I don't know, Debra. That's God's decision. He is merciful and forgiving, but He is also just, and unrepented sin is not tolerated. We could only warn them, as my father did for over one hundred years. And you heard him try to explain the coming catastrophe to you family many times. They just wouldn't listen. We couldn't force them, eventually everyone needs to make their own decision."

Debra was crying into her hands. *I was beginning to accept my family's destruction as their choice and now this! Why is Zalith allowed to practice her evil, bloodthirsty goddess worship when my sisters were destroyed? Maybe Shem can help me with this, give me an answer, or even just hold me. But should I even tell Shem? Tell anyone? After all, the child is dead; nothing could bring it back. Revealing its* sacrifice *would only bring strife and we have enough strife and tension as it is. Shouldn't I make sure she is punished? But would they believe me? It would be my word against Zalith's. Everyone thinks Zalith is the model of purity and innocence. She has them all fooled, even my husband. I never trusted her, not at all. She's always had a double personality. Always so much more knowledgeable about sensual pleasures than she pretends when Noah or Naamah are around, always giggling and making sexual jokes. No wonder she hinted that she and Ham were going to ignore Noah's command for abstinence.*

"Well we are young. Noah can't expect us to abstain for long can he? I mean… it is asking a lot from my husband, isn't it?" She looked down admirably at herself, her hands skimming down her slender yet voluptuous body. Without saying it exactly, she was implying that she was so desirable, how could Ham resist her, while it was no great feat for Shem and Japheth to obey their father's command.

"But Zalith, what if you conceive?" she and her other sister-in-law, Cassia asked simultaneously. Zalith just smiled that superior, all-knowing smile she had given them all too often when the three girls were alone. When the others were present, she was quick to conceal that smirk, and was the model of obedience. Now Debra knew what that smile meant: she was already pregnant.

More than once, Debra had caught Shem's eye while he looked admirably at Zalith. She had been halfway kidding when she pretended to be jealous. She trusted him, but he must have been feeling at least a little guilty to protest so much.

Now they will all see I've been right all along. But should I tell them? Should I confront Zalith? I'll tell Shem in the morning. Surely he won't let this evil persist. She fell into a troubled sleep, filled with dreams of temple sacrifices.

Chapter 3
The Ark, 2348 BC

"Debra! Wake up! There is work to do!" Debra half-heard the voices of her husband and in-laws. She wasn't sure if she was asleep or awake; the voices seemed close, but became distant and muffled, and then all too close again. She opened her eyes to see them standing above her. Ham was smiling and laughing, the others looked concerned. She didn't see Zalith.

"Debra", her mother-in-law was saying, "we are all under a lot of pressure, but really dear, drinking isn't the answer." She sounded concerned and a little shocked at Debra's apparent lack of decorum, but Debra really had no idea what she was talking about.

She looked at her blankly. Her brother-in-laws gave each other knowing looks, confusing Debra even more. Then she realized where she was, lying in a disheveled heap, in the storage room where they kept the wine. Her eyes were red and her head hurt. She knew it was from crying for hours, but she could tell that the rest of the family blamed the empty wine cask beside her. *As usual, I am always in the wrong place at the wrong time.* She heard Japheth and Shem talking in the background, they were going to have to somehow keep the wine room locked, for Debra's' own good.

The atmosphere at breakfast was strained to say the least. Everyone was being condescendingly nice to her.

Noah started to pray. It was probably his normal voice but to Debra's ringing ears he sounded like he was talking through a towel. She heard enough to be glad she didn't quite hear the rest.

"… and dear Lord, please protect and heal Debra. Amen."

She couldn't eat the porridge of grain, dried fruit, and fresh cream that she usually relished. She felt more than saw all of her relatives again exchanging knowing glances. She wanted to knock Ham's silly smirk off his face. *How can he be amused at anything when his child has just been murdered by its own mother? He must know. Oh! That couldn't have been Ham's baby. They have not been married that long. Zalith must have been pregnant when she showed up at Noah's compound.*

"Debra, Honey, just eat a little, it will make you feel better. I know when my brothers…" Naamah didn't finish her sentence, but Debra could imagine she was going to recommend something to help a hangover.

Zalith was there, looking fresh and as innocent as ever, making Debra feel even more self-conscious and un-attractive. Debra's face was red and puffy, as she wasn't up to performing her usual morning beauty routine.

"You know, I wasn't drinking. Really. I thought that I heard a lamb or kid crying and…"

Ham interrupted, "And you were looking for it in the wine room?" He and Zalith started to laugh; most of the others smiled. Debra glared at Shem and was relieved that he at least didn't think that remark was funny.

"No, I.." *What good will it do for me to protest? They think I was drunk and won't believe anything I say, anyway.*

"Of course dear, the alco- person with a problem- is always the last to realize that there is a problem, " Naamah gently, but firmly, explained.

"We will get you through this, with God's help, of course."

"Debra, I will gladly help you in any way that I can". Zalith sweetly said.

That was the last straw; Debra curtly excused herself and went to her room. In a few moments Shem arrived.

"Honey, if I had known you had a drinking problem, I would have tried to help you. I wish you would have confided in me and maybe I could have spared you this embarrassment."

"But Shem, I wasn't drunk, let me tell you what happened."

He just went on talking as if he were repeating a carefully thought out speech with no room for interruptions. "Of course, I knew at least one of the others on board was over-imbibing, because the limited supply of wine was dwindling faster than the one glass at dinner for each of us would explain. Don't worry. We all care for you and we have made a pact to never leave you alone, to try to keep you occupied and content. Zalith has thoughtfully volunteered to help you with the afternoon chores, even though we all know how much she dislikes working with the animals. Wasn't that nice of her?"

That was enough. She was crying and kicking her feet like a spoiled child. Of course she knew this didn't help her case, but it was so frustrating! *Men were frustrating! Couldn't he see what Zalith was trying to do?*

She tried to calm down enough to blurt out some of the scene she had accidentally stumbled upon last night. She was having difficulty making him understand amidst her anger and her tears. She was even more frustrated when she did finally communicate what happened that Shem reacted with disbelief.

"Debra, I know you wouldn't make up such a thing, but are you sure?"

"Shem, believe me, something absolutely horrible happened last night and Zalith was at the root of it. She isn't as innocent as you think."

"Okay, Debra, I can see you at least believe that something bad happened. Don't mention it to anyone else; my parents have enough to worry about. I will talk to Ham as soon as possible and try to get to the bottom of this."

***

Shem was relieved the rain finally stopped. As the ship's timekeeper, he tracked the days and nights of the storm at exactly forty, just as God had promised. For many weeks after the torrential rainstorm, the wind and the waves tossed the massive ship around under a turbulent sky. Now patchy areas of sunshine broke through the clouds and the Ark residents were occasionally able to walk on the deck.

He once again marveled at the wisdom and forethought of his mother to insist that a deck even be built. After the foretold long rainstorm, she knew a deck would be useful not only for relaxation, but water storage, herb growing, and fishing. She said it would be easy to construct once the rain was over, turning the roof of the second story into the floor. They could make it level, now that the slope was not needed for drainage. They cut a door and used the wood she had insisted they bring to build a railing. *She was always planning and looking to the future. What faith she has, to believe that they could even expect a future after witnessing such destruction.* Now that the deck was built, they were able to again enjoy the sun and fresh air.

Sometimes the air didn't smell all that fresh. There were floating masses of intertwined decaying vegetation often carrying the rotting remains of some animal. Shem tried not to think about how the rest of the earth had perished so suddenly. *I know I should just be grateful to God for our salvation, but was all that destruction really necessary? Wasn't there some other way?* He asked himself for the millionth time. He knew that he should trust God; His decisions were holy and beyond man's understanding. Shem kept his doubts to himself. He led the group

21

in their scripture studies and he felt it was his place to set a good example. He knew these issues especially bothered Debra, she had heard her family begging her to let them in as the Ark began to float. Maybe those memories were the source of her secret drinking. He saw Ham standing alone by the railing and decided this would be a good time to talk to him.

"Ham, can I talk to you about a serious matter?"

"Sure Shem, we seem to have nothing but work and time."

"This is difficult, so I am going to be blunt. Debra said she saw Zalith sacrificing an infant to an idol and then Debra heard her throw the body overboard."

Ham's face clouded over and his ever-present smile faded. "Shem! You surely don't believe her? Zalith would never do such a thing!"

His face became even sadder. "There was a baby. We kept Zalith's pregnancy a secret not to upset Mom and Dad. We knew when the baby was born they would welcome it joyfully, but we just weren't ready for the endless lectures about self-restraint and responsibility they were sure to give us. You know how sensitive Zalith is. I didn't want to upset her in her condition. Anyway, it wasn't her fault. I was the weak one. But sadly, Zalith delivered too early, and the baby was stillborn. What Debra saw was Zalith's dedication of the small body to God, and prayers for his soul and her physical and emotional healing. Why would Debra think otherwise? I was there for the prayers, but I slipped back to our room before the burial. I just couldn't bear it. I suppose in Debra's state of delirium, she imagined Zalith doing those awful things. And Shem, even without the wine, we both know how spiteful and jealous women can be. Especially when one of them is a s beautiful as Zalith"

Ham's lip began to tremble and he was having difficulty speaking. He avoided Shem's eyes as he told him, "Shem, please don't mention this to the others. Zalith and I are in enough pain, without everyone's sympathy constantly reminding us. And can you imagine the reproaches from Mom and Dad? Zalith is just not up to that. We want to forget and look forward to our future children." Ham's lip quivered even more and tears started to pour down his face.

Shem gave him a brotherly embrace and turned away. He never was one for tearful shows of emotion. *I suppose I would be crying if it had been my child .*The tears brought back thoughts of the effeminate men he had seen Ham associate with in the city. Shem often wondered about Ham's choice of friends. He was sure that Ham was too innocent to

22

realize the probable sexual preference of many of the young men of his acquaintance. They seemed nice enough that day he joined them for lunch at Ham's invitation; and not prone to the drunkenness and violence of the more "manly" types.

Shem thought that he was going to have to speak to Ham about his companions, but their father soon decided to cut off all social ties with the city, so that unpleasant conversation never happened. From that time on, their only contact with the city was Noah's preaching and an occasional shopping trip to obtain the supplies they could not grow or otherwise make. Besides, Shem hadn't doubted Ham's attraction to women for a long time, not since he had seen how he acted around Zalith.

Chapter 4
The Ark, 2348 BC

Debra was diligently raking out the sheep pens and putting down fresh straw for their bedding. She really didn't mind taking care of the animals. The routine was comforting and they did seem to like her. Being a city girl, she didn't have a lot of experience with animals but she was learning everyday. Noah only assigned her the care of the calm, gentle animals, while the more boisterous, possibly dangerous animals' care was left for Cassia and the men. They were much more experienced in that area. Debra wondered at their ability to seemingly communicate with such a wide variety of animals. She didn't really understand, but was glad that they were able to care for everything from hippos to lions. She would stick with the farm animals.

Thoughts of her life in the city, Tymorrah, were mostly unpleasant so she tried not to dwell on them. But thinking with affection of Shem, her mind wandered back to the time she had first met him. She was upset, and bolted blindly through one of the alleys and literally ran right into him as he was leaving the backdoor of a shop. The impact sent her flying, landing in the dust of the street. Shem helped her up. He seemed genuinely concerned and asked her what was wrong.

"Is someone chasing you? Do you need some help?"

By his clothes and his gentle attitude she knew he must be one of the religious fanatics living outside the city. Most of the men of Tymorrah would have just laughed at her, or worse, taken advantage of her. Usually, a woman alone in a back street was fair game, but she hadn't thought of that when she started running, so upset and distracted she didn't know exactly where she was or how she got there. Shem tried to get her to calm down, to tell him what was wrong so he could help her. She could only blurt out broken words and parts of sentences. He took her to a small café around the corner, bought her a refreshing fruit drink and tried again to get her to calm down.

"You just don't know," she started to tell him, but broke down in tears again, "you can't know of the horrible things that are done in the name of religion." She tried to become a little more composed and went on. "My sister, Lana, recently married and was expecting her first child. Last night, she and her husband came to my parent's house very excited. They said that they had wonderful news."

More tears, and then she stammered on with her story, "the sacrificial committee had visited my sister and brother-in-law and told them that their unborn child had been selected as the sacrifice of honor for today's great feast in reverence of Inanna. I couldn't believe what I was hearing. How could they be joyful over this news? I never could bear the sacrifices; I always turned my head. I went to the rites. Everybody went. But I never dreamed my sister would give up her own child to be publicly murdered, and for what, a stone image? Lana saw the horror on my face. 'What's wrong Debra, aren't you happy for us?'

'Of course not! How could you!' I said.

'Debra, it is an honor for our family. We all get to sit at the royal table during the celebration. Don't you know that this will be guaranteed eternal salvation for our child? It will transcend to Heaven to be personally raised by Inanna. If we refuse, the goddess will punish us, and our city, for not granting her wish. Besides, the sacrificial committee will pay us very well. Our future children will be wealthy. You know we were wondering how to support a family so soon after marriage'

'But Lana', I protested, 'the child isn't even born yet'

'That is the best part! The priestesses will, well actually I have already taken the first dose, give me a medication, a powder to make me go into labor. When the pains start, sometime in the morning, they are going to give me another drug to make me sleep. The delivery will be painless and I don't even have to see the child. The priestesses said they could keep me in a euphoric state the whole day, maybe even longer if I want them to supply the necessary medications. They said that would be best because sometimes the mothers forget what a privilege it is and try to change their minds. The drugs will prevent that kind of dishonor.'

I was horrified, but the rest of my family was jubilant. The last thing I heard before I ran to my room was my father asking 'just how much money?'

When my parents and my other sisters were leaving to go to the festival, I couldn't do it. I turned and ran the other way, and that's when I plowed into you." Debra remembered the kindness in his eyes like it was yesterday.

"No wonder you are so upset."

Shem thoughtfully sipped his drink and then gently told her, "There is a better way, there is only One True God, a living God, not a man-made image, One who does not ask for human sacrifices, only sacrifices of love and obedience. When you are up to it, I will visit you and your family and try to convince them of the urgency of leaving Tymorrah." Shem then walked her to her parent's house and promised to return soon.

That was the beginning of their courtship and Shem and Noah's unsuccessful attempt to convert her family.

In the middle of her sheep-pen reverie, she was startled to hear Shem speaking. He had quietly walked up behind her. She could feel the tension in his voice as he slowly explained his theory of what had happened in the storage room with Zalith.

"Debra, I think I have it figured out. Ham told me Zalith did deliver a premature stillborn child and that they just wanted a quiet, private funeral. I believe that when you saw Zalith, your mind, not being quite in a normal state, confused reality with the ever-present memories of your sister and her child. Promise me two things and I think we can work this out. Stop dwelling on the past, and stop over-indulging. The alcohol might make you feel better temporarily, but in the end it just intensifies your emotions and grief over your family."

Debra let out a long hard sigh, closing her eyes and biting her lip to prevent another angry outburst. She knew it was useless to protest over her sobriety that night; and maybe Shem was right. Maybe her imagination and her memories were clouding her interpretations of what she had seen.

"All right, Shem, I will try to put the past behind me, and I will never drink wine again." Even though she knew she had not been drinking, she wanted to reassure her husband. Things were certainly not the same between them since his family had discovered her in the wine room.

Shem smiled the same big warm but somehow still serious grin that had made her instantly trust him that day they met in Tymorrah.

"Now that's more like the strong woman I married. I need to get back to my chores and let you finish yours. I'll see you at dinner," He kissed her on the cheek and walked away. She could see that his spirits were visibly lifted to hear such a positive response from her.

Debra smiled as she watched him go. Her smile faded as she turned back to the sheep and told them confidentially, "Still, I know what I saw. I know what I heard. But I can't let that woman come between Shem and me."

The sheep didn't answer, another reason she liked spending time with them.

Chapter 6
The Ark, 2348 BC

Zalith had always known she had a special destiny. Her mother, the king's favorite wife and High Priestess of the temple of Inanna, often talked of how Zalith's star chart foretold that she would be "The One". Her mother wasn't exactly sure what that meant, that part was still to be revealed. But now Zalith was sure: her special destiny was to preserve the sacred knowledge from those who meant to destroy it.

The irony of using the Ark of Noah to save her image of Inanna and sacred books of spells and drug formulations was not lost on her. She knew that Noah and his family thought they were spared because they still practiced the old religion, and that the destruction was from their God, Jehovah. She wasn't entirely convinced that the Flood was from Jehovah, although she admitted He was powerful and that Noah was in direct communication with Him.

She couldn't quite understand why Inanna, the Earth Mother, allowed this Flood. If Jehovah alone was responsible, then He surely was a jealous God, as Noah called Him. *Just like a man, destroying His own creation so that no one else could enjoy it. I suppose the point was to destroy all the other gods as well as their worshippers, while only Jehovah's worshippers survived.* Her smile widened to a grin, once again reflecting on the irony of the situation.

Although she didn't have all the answers, she had her theories. Noah said that the Flood was a purification of violence from the world, the violence that was personified in the giants that terrorized country and city alike. She was sure Noah was wrong. Perhaps the Flood had natural causes: maybe one of the stars of heaven fell, colliding with the earth, piercing the earth's protective covering of water, and causing the downpour.

Zalith believed that all spirits, including Jehovah could see into the future. Wanting to warn and protect Noah, He had him build the Ark. Then Jehovah convinced Noah the coming destruction was His plan. *If He truly was the creator God, why didn't He just re-create man and all of the plants and animals as He claims to have done in the first place? Then all traces of my religion would have vanished as well. The very fact that I am here makes me think this Jehovah isn't in as much control as Noah and Naamah think.*

A slight smile crossed her face again. *Natural causes for the disaster would have been the explanation given by the professors and scientists at the University in Tymorrah; that is if they weren't all dead. Their chemistry and their mathematics didn't save them*; now almost laughing to herself and remembering her instructor's vain attempts to convince her that science was the only source of truth. *Silly men, denying the existence of the gods and the power in the movements of the stars didn't make their actuality any less, or their powers diminished. Their lectures on planetary motion and formulas for orbits didn't do much to change anything or to save them. Ah, but there is a reason for everything. I know the Earth itself, possibly even the universe, is somehow responsible for this deluge. The Spirit of Mother Eve, and the other ancient, natural forces are working together to mold a new earth and make it ready for their favorite earthly being, me. My descendants and I will reign on earth for eternity, and at some point in time I will merge into The Vast Oneness when my spirit is perfected.*

Zalith wasn't afraid of death; she knew there was eternity for the spirit. That's why she didn't mourn for her parents and her friends. That's why she didn't mourn for her child. They would all be reunited in eternal spiritual communion, living in what her mother called 'Nirvana' forever.

Zalith hadn't seen too much wrong with the old earth. Even though the reason for this disaster was unclear to her now, she was sure that knowledge would be revealed to her eventually. Her voices would tell her, the same voices that had asked her for her child. They must be obeyed: she had no choice.

She was sure her decision not to tell Ham the whole truth about the baby was justified. He didn't need to know that she had induced the miscarriage with herbs, nor that the child had been born alive and she had to smother it. A sacrifice while still alive would have been too noisy anyway. She wasn't yet sure that she had total control of Ham. She could feel her husband's reluctance to total submission to her and her religion, but she was sure she would eventually attain his complete subjugation.

Zalith continued to embroider a silver star as she thought about Ham and his family. It wasn't that she didn't like her husband's parents; they were nice enough to her. *But how can they be so narrow-minded? She didn't deny that their God existed, but how could He be the only one? How could He claim to have created the earth, the moon and the stars?* She knew better. She had been trained from an early age in all of the sacred mysteries. She wasn't like the scientists who denied the supernatural. Zalith knew for a fact the spirit world existed and that it had always existed. Supernatural entities, the Earth Mother, the god of the wind, the god of the waters, and others not yet known guided the creation of the world, from simple to complex. Everything in the world had its own life force and searched for its own expression and place in time. The search for that unique place continued until it was found, even if it took innumerable eons. Her voices reassured her that she was right.

She had often acted as the medium the spirits used to communicate to the living during the séances her mother conducted. The voices came from beyond time, claiming to be older than even Adam. They came from a peaceful, pleasant world. The individual spirits were separate; yet still part of the Wholeness of Eternity. After death, time and eternity would blend beyond her present human understanding, the séances only giving her and the others a glimpse. She wondered with happy anticipation when her mother's spirit would try to contact her. She had confidently promised Zalith she would.

Zalith wasn't just another young follower of the many faces of Inanna, the Warrior Princess, the Huntress and the Mother of us all. She was personally trained by her own mother, the high priestess, Dehlia, in the arts of the secret sisterhood. There was great power in the "higher knowledge", the knowledge only those initiated into the highest temple circles were allowed to learn.

The ins and outs of what her in-laws called witchcraft were taught to her and the other young students at the temple, but only the most gifted were allowed to study further, to eventually become priestesses as she and her mother were. Now she was the only human left with such knowledge. Ham had helped her hide her herbs, medications, candles, books, and robes. He laughed as she respectfully carried her statue of Inanna, not letting him, a man and an unbeliever, touch the sacred image. He was invaluable in helping her sneak everything on board, yet why he still distanced himself from her religion, she didn't know. On the other hand, he didn't really worship God either. Neither did he deny His existence. Ham liked to cover all the bases. Yes, he had chosen the safety of the Ark. What was the harm, he had told her. If his father were right, he had chosen correctly; if his father was crazy, he would just move to Tymorrah with her. She smiled and told the eight-pointed star emblem emerging on her robe,

"Ham did love the city."

She remembered when they had met. Of course it wasn't as accidental as Ham believed. She sought him out and contrived to make their meeting appear casual. Earlier that week, she and her mother had been shopping in the city. She fondly remembered that sometimes they would put on common clothes and just have a girls' day-out. The royal guards were never far away, sometimes dressed in disguises as well, just in case someone tried to harm them.

There was a commotion in the street outside the fabric shop as they were leaving. Someone was standing on a platform and giving a speech. It was Noah again, with another one of those 'end-of-the-world-is-coming' speeches. Death and destruction were imminent, but Noah was offering salvation for those who would join him.

Most of the crowd were laughing and jeering. Some listened but still turned away. Zalith could sense their embarrassment. Of course they didn't want anyone else to know they were tempted to believe him. Zalith turned with a smile to enjoy the moment with her mother, but her mother wasn't smiling. Zalith thought Dehlia was taking this speech way too seriously. *Surely she didn't believe this man.* They didn't talk much on the way back to the palace. Zalith tried to make some small talk about the quality of the silks they had purchased, but her mother wasn't listening. She was deep in thought, almost in one of her trances.

The next morning as she was leaving the breakfast room, Zalith's mother motioned for her to come near to her. "Dear, I need to talk to you about something very serious; meet me in our secret room in thirty minutes."

There wasn't a lot of privacy in the palace, but her mother had shown her a room in the cellar only accessible through a hidden back staircase. When she arrived Dehlia was deep in prayer, talking with the voices that only she could hear.

As Dehlia finished she turned to her, "Zalith, there was something real about that man yesterday. You need to find a way to get on that boat. Someone in our family, the royal family, has to survive to carry on our blood and our ways."

"But mother, even if I wanted to, even if I believed there was some bit of truth in Noah's speech, they are not going to allow me to join them, a priestess of Inanna."

"Of course not. You have to deceive them in some way. I have been doing some checking. The youngest son of the Preacher often comes into town to enjoy the pleasures of the city, probably without his parents' knowledge. You need to meet him and make him fall in love with you. He will be your ticket to board that boat."

Chapter 7

Tymorrah, October 2349 BC

Zalith was pleasantly surprised when she found the Preacher's son. She half expected just a younger version of the old man. She feared that he would be eccentric, with his father's wild beard and hair, no sense of fashion, and worst of all, boring. But Ham was anything but boring.

She had made some inquiries, of course in one of her disguises. The royal princess shouldn't be out hobnobbing with the commoners, seeking the whereabouts of religious fanatics. Her disguises were fun, and she almost never was recognized, especially if she wore a wig to cover her trademark blond hair. The informants told her to go to the square and look for the tallest, best built man there, with dark skin, short curly black hair, and a fashionably clean-shaven, handsome face. Well, that was encouraging. At least he wasn't ugly. She thought she would rather drown than get involved with an ugly man.

Zalith easily found the man they described sitting at a table drinking and laughing with some of his buddies. She started to approach the table and then suddenly stopped as she recognized the garb of his companions. *Were they the ...? Yes, male for male prostitutes from the temple. Well, maybe this wasn't going to be so easy if Ham leaned in that direction.*

She knew that many men and women were bi-sexual. Even the older priestesses had encouraged her and the other young women of the temple to experiment. And then maybe, although unlikely, those men were just his friends and not his lovers. She faded into a shadowy corner to compose herself and re-think this project. Zalith decided to attempt the seduction anyway; what would her mother think if she failed? *He is handsome and apparently knows how to enjoy himself.* Not at all the stuffy religious fanatic she had originally expected. Ham was magnetic. Everyone near his table in the square seemed to be fascinated with him. It was almost as if he were holding court like her father did to allow foreign dignitaries to kowtow to him. Only Ham's court was entirely voluntary. Everyone around him hung on his every word. They smiled when he smiled and laughed when he laughed.

Zalith put on her best lost-and-innocent look and "accidentally" walked backwards into their table. She apologized while helping them clean up their drinks. "I am so sorry. I seem to have lost my friends. I don't really want to be alone here. Can I wait for them with you?" she hesitantly asked.

"Sure, Sweetie. You'll be safe with us, " One of the male prostitutes said in a purposely effeminate voice.

She pretended not to notice the confidential glances the temple-ites exchanged with that last comment. They seemed to ignore her, but Ham was immediately interested. She started to relax and engage him in conversation without revealing too much of her identity. She glanced at the old-fashioned robes lying on the chair behind him.

Before she asked, Ham told her, "Those are mine. I have to put them on and leave soon, so that I can get home before my parents wake up.

"Are you related to the Preacher, the one who is always tormenting the city with his doom and gloom messages?"

Ham laughed, "Yes, he is my father. You know, my identity is always good for a conversation opener, and it seems you townspeople are delighted to help corrupt the Preacher's son. Knowing that Noah is my father is usually good for a few party invitations. Everyone is happy to help me hide my secret city-life; they think it is a tremendous joke on the old man who constantly preaches repentance to them."

Before they shared several drinks, Ham motioned to the others that he wanted to have some privacy. The tempelites and the other men and women gathered around Ham's table glanced knowingly at him before they moved away and busied themselves with their own sexual conquests. Zalith kept the conversation casual, flirting just enough to keep his gaze totally riveted on her. She was triumphantly relieved that he was attracted to her and wanted to meet her again tomorrow night. He said good-bye and took off at a gentle jog to get home before the sun rose.

"Honey, you had better let us walk you home," one of Ham's prostitute companions told her.

"Don't worry. I can take care of myself" Zalith replied, thinking that they would be of little help anyway. Her words were prophetic; during her walk back to the palace, a shadowy figure rushed from behind her. She instinctively dodged his attack by ducking her shoulder and catching him in the stomach with a hard blow from her elbow. The attacker was still bent over, the wind knocked out of him, when Zalith hit him with a double fisted blow to the back of the neck. He crumbled and Zalith triumphantly left. Without looking back, she heard a reassuring thud as his head hit the cobblestones and she knew he wouldn't be attacking anyone else that night or possibly ever again. Fortunately, all of Inanna's priestesses were trained in the arts of war, the hunt, and self-defense.

***

Ham was relieved but amazed that his parents accepted Zalith for what she appeared to be, an innocent young woman seeking refuge from the wickedness of the city. He fondly remembered their passionate and romantic courtship, even if it was short. They would meet at a predetermined location and spend hours together: talking, laughing and usually ending the evening by renting a room for a few hours at one of the inns near the town square. He was so in love with her that for the first time the sexual part of the relationship seemed secondary. Of course he enjoyed it, everything about their lovemaking was perfect as far as he was concerned and she seemed to enjoy it as much as he did. He had never felt this way about anyone before. His feelings for her were a level above sexual, a level he never expected to experience.

One night about three weeks into their relationship, he met her at their usual table in the lobby of her favorite inn. But this time she wasn't alone, her mother was waiting with Zalith. Ham and Dehlia instantly hit it off. She found him absolutely charming and he was fascinated by her elegance and self-assurance, although his strict upbringing made him feel a little uncomfortable chitchatting with his lover's mother. When Dehlia told him about Zalith's true identity he was speechless. He was amazed that the royal princess was running around town incognito and having a love affair with him, of all people.

"Don't you think all this clandestine activity could be dangerous for your daughter?" Ham asked.

Dehlia laughed. "There are guards all around, and they have been watching over the two of you since Zalith had the run-in with a would be attacker the night you met. If you had made one false or inappropriate move, your life would have ended."

Ham wondered what an inappropriate move was, if it wasn't spending the night with Zalith in a downtown hotel. Dehlia told him that from now on, there would be no more hotels. Ham was crestfallen, believing that Dehlia wanted Zalith to break off the relationship, but she continued to explain that they should just meet in Zalith's quarters.

"It will be so much more comfortable and safer as well," Dehlia said.

He couldn't believe his good luck when Zalith agreed to marry him, to live with him and his eccentric family. He wasn't entirely sure when or even if he brought up the idea of marriage. He hadn't even dared to think she would marry him, but Zalith started talking wedding plans. He was shocked, confused, and started to tell her to slow down, but stopped himself. *If such a beautiful and powerful member of the royal family wants* to *marry me, why shouldn't I marry her?* He was ready to give up his family, their values and their God. But Zalith didn't want that. She wanted to live with him and his family and give up all the grandeur of the palace and the honor due to her as princess and the future high priestess. Ham knew her current pious attitude of reverence to Jehovah was just an act, so his family would accept her. Therefore, the attraction to the Ark must have been himself, and only him. Surely she had not believed his father's preaching.

Ham and Dehlia agreed that his parents would likely not accept Zalith as readily if they knew her true identity, or at least view her as daughter-in-law potential. Ham was surprised that Dehlia so quickly accepted her daughter's marriage to a commoner, let alone one with such a crazy family. He didn't understand, but he wasn't going to complain. Dehlia told him she thought their marriage was meant to be, foretold in the stars. She explained that Ham's mother was actually her own cousin, so Ham too was of the royal family of Cain, and not just a commoner. Dehlia personally arranged their elopement, even though they had to keep it a secret from everyone else, especially Zalith's father. They were married during a secret civil ceremony held in the secluded room in the palace basement. Dehlia knew there was no other way for her to be able to witness her daughter's wedding, and she told Ham she could always arrange for any untrustworthy witnesses to conveniently disappear.

Ham wished the ceremony could have been in a more romantic setting, perhaps a forest glen, with sunlight trickling down through the trees as they made their vows, but Dehlia insisted on as much secrecy as possible.

Their second marriage ceremony later performed by Methuselah was also small. None of Zalith's imaginary or real family was invited, and Methuselah and Noah's family were the only ones left on earth practicing the exclusive worship of Jehovah. Ham didn't care about the lack of guests: he was as entranced by her beauty when he lifted her veil to kiss her as he was the night they met.

Ham handpicked the clothes she wore the night she arrived at their family compound. If she had worn one of her customarily fashionable, but rather immodest outfits, Noah and Naamah may not have been so sympathetic when she appeared seemingly out of nowhere in the middle of the night. In actuality, Zalith's mother and two of the palace guards dropped her off, and waited nearby in the shadows until Noah opened the gate and let her in.

Zalith had torn her clothes and dirtied her face and body to make it appear as if she had been wildly running through the brush before she began frantically banging on the gates of the family compound.

"Come in child. What is troubling you?" Noah asked. The rest of the family started to gather around.

"Oh, Sir, thank you for letting me in! My father! How could he! I thought he loved me! But he sold me to the temple authorities, to be one of the temple prosti... well you know. I can't even say the word. I didn't know where else to go. I heard you preaching in town and ..."

"There, there dear, just try to calm down. You are safe here."

Zalith took a deep breath and continued, "When my father told me I was to report to the temple in the morning, that he would personally take me there, I was horrified. I couldn't face such a life, so I secretly left, sneaking out after everyone else was asleep. God must have been watching over me, to get me through Tymorrah and all of its many night dangers. I remembered hearing your invitation to flee the wickedness of the city and seek safety with you and your family." Zalith glanced around at the family, with not even a tiny trace of recognition as her eyes skimmed past Ham. *What an actress*, Ham thought admirably. He hoped his own actions wouldn't give them away.

Chapter 8

Tymorrah, November 2349, BC

"Of course we will take care of you!" Noah said to the pretty and distraught young woman standing in his courtyard. He almost couldn't contain his excitement: his preaching had finally brought a convert to them. God's hand was surely in this. *My youngest son is still in need of a wife, and maybe…well that may come in due time, if it is God's will.*

"Thank God you have arrived safely," Noah didn't even want to think about the dangers of the city she had just escaped. *That place was bad enough in the day, but a woman alone at night?* He consciously blocked any visualization from his imagination about what could have happened. Her arrival truly must have been a miracle in itself.

"What can we do for you? Are you hungry? Thirsty?"

Zalith sweetly smiled and said, "I would like to just get cleaned up and rest. I am worn out."

"Debra, can she…what is your name dear?" Noah asked

"Zalith"

"Debra, can you loan Zalith some clean clothes? Someone will need to take her into town tomorrow to buy some until Naamah has time to make some. We can't have our new family member wearing rags, now can we."

"Naamah, please show her to one of the guest rooms. We can talk more tomorrow."

***

God has answered my prayers and sent a daughter to me, and a wife for my youngest, Naamah thought joyfully to herself as she readied the room for Zalith. *Maybe this pious young girl will keep Ham home and stop his secret nighttime wanderings.*

Naamah didn't tell Ham, or Noah, that she knew Ham often slipped out of the house, returning just in time to get a few hours of sleep. She hated deceit, but she didn't want Noah's reaction to Ham's city-life leading to an emotional rift between them. Ham's life was too important to her. She didn't want to take any chances he would not be on the Ark. She covered for him, made excuses for his exhaustion. Compromise was against her nature, but she didn't see any other way to avoid a violent confrontation that might lead to Ham's leaving home and rejecting the safety of the Ark. Surely Ham would see the corruption of Tymorrah as God's judgment was fulfilled. She was convinced the demonstration of

God's power and His love for them would turn Ham away forever from a life obsessed with temporary pleasures.

Chapter 9

The Ark, April 2348 BC

"Noah, I want a divorce." Zara's matter-of-fact statement still sliced through his heart and soul even after one hundred and twenty years. Noah tried to shake the memory of his first wife from his head as he walked on the deck in the cool night air. The waters were beginning to recede and soon they would disembark to start a new life. He tried to concentrate on that new life and new world in which he and Naamah would live, but thoughts of the past kept creeping into his mind. He had loved Zara dearly.

Noah knew she was the one when they first met at her cousin's wedding. *Didn't she love me? Was it all an act?* He couldn't believe that Zara had never loved him. He couldn't erase their nights of passion, their intimate moments. He also couldn't erase the pain of her re-marriage so soon after their divorce. That hurt. It made the breakup so final. Until then, he maintained hopes of winning her back. He desperately wanted to convince her that he wasn't crazy, that God did speak to him. Now she was gone forever, her and their children, killed in the deluge. Noah let the night wind dry his tears as he finished sipping down the remainder of the wine cask. He threw the empty container overboard and quietly slipped back to bed to let the wine lull him into a deep slumber of forgetfulness.

***

Naamah lay silently as Noah came back into their room. She almost said something to him, almost asked him why he couldn't sleep but stopped herself. If he wanted to talk about whatever was bothering him, he wouldn't be trying so hard not to wake her. She knew anyway. She also knew when he was lost in his memories; there was nothing she could really do to ease his pain over Zara. Naamah was jealous of Zara; she really didn't want to be, but she couldn't help it. Noah told her when they first became betrothed that he didn't think he could ever love anyone the way he had loved Zara, but he promised to be a good husband to her. And that he was.

Yes, she was jealous of Zara. How can one compete with a memory? But she also admired Noah for his devotion to his first wife, it was part of the reason she loved him so much. Few men could love a woman for a century with no hope of that love being returned. Most men in her town went through wives like shoes. But she couldn't blame just the men; the women were always searching for new partners as well, neither sex honored their marriage vows. Many marriages ended after a few years in divorce, followed rapidly by a new marriage. Or sometimes like her father, Lamech, men had several wives at the same time. Polygamy didn't shock anyone anymore and often was deemed necessary since the violent wars had decimated the male population. But Naamah knew it wasn't God's plan.

Naamah had never met a man like Noah, capable of such love, and with such deep emotions. Noah's love for Zara was part of Noah and she learned to accept it as she had accepted every other part of him. She only hoped that one day she too could be the recipient of such love.

She knew Noah married her more from necessity than romance. They joked that their marriage was "truly a match made in heaven"; since they were the only man and woman alive still worshiping Jehovah as the one true God. She also knew it was God who brought them together, not the matchmaking efforts of her brother, Tubal-cain. But she let her brother think her marriage was his doing.

Tubal-cain was so happy to finally see her with a man. He returned one day from a distant job making some metal hinges and door handles. He didn't really need the money and seldom traveled so far from home to work anymore, but he was curious to see the boat that everyone was talking about. He had heard rumors that a crazy prophet was building a giant boat, miles away from any body of water. When a messenger came from Noah requesting help for some metal work, he decided to take the job himself, even though one of his apprentices would have been the obvious choice.

He walked into the large reading room where she was studying and announced jokingly. "Hey Naamy, I finally found someone as crazy as you. Do you want me to fix you up?"

From habit, her heart sank. Her brothers were always trying to "fix her up" with someone and she was tired of the disappointment she experienced after every encounter. She knew it was unusual for a woman of her advancing years not to be married. At four hundred, she was almost past child bearing and was despairing of finding a mate. It wasn't that she didn't have any offers. She knew she was attractive enough, but not one man she met measured up to her standards. Still, she was hopeful, God had promised her she would have children and in fact be the mother of many future peoples.

Once she almost accepted an offer of marriage from a friend of her brother, Jubal. The suitor said he loved her, and she was so lonely! While deep in prayer, asking God if this man was the one she should marry, an angel appeared to her. He told her to be patient, for in time she would marry and only she and her family would be saved from a worldwide flood. But that was over one hundred years ago, and still she waited. Had God forgotten her? Was the angel just a dream?

After hearing more about Noah, her spirits were lifted and she was finding it difficult to contain her emotions. She knew that this boat builder must be the promised one or somehow connected to the man God wanted her to marry. How else would he know of the impending disaster, if not from God? She certainly had not told anyone. Her family thought that she was crazy enough. She agreed to return with Tubal-cain on his next visit to Noah.

While anxiously awaiting the trip, Naamah kept herself busy, but Noah and his mission were constantly on her mind. She was a teacher in her brothers' town instructing her many nieces and nephews in the schoolhouse that Tubal-cain built. She did her best to prepare the children for the university in Tymorrah, which they would attend when they became teenagers. She felt honored that her brothers and sisters-in-law trusted her with their children's education. Sadly, most of the time it did seem that she took the education of the young ones more seriously than their parents did. Her brothers asked that she keep her fanatic religious views to herself and not burden the children with them.

She was allowed to tell them the creation story, but she was instructed to present it as that, a fanciful story. Her brothers believed that absolute morals and even absolute truths were old-fashioned and only served to give the children unnecessary feelings of guilt when they grew up into normal adults, doing normal adult activities.

It was truly a tragedy that her brothers were so morally lax. Even so, they could have accepted a place on the Ark, but they only laughed at her and Noah when they tried to convince them of the impending catastrophe. Her brothers weren't very spiritual; in fact they largely rejected the existence of the supernatural. They believed that the present world was all that existed. They did not believe in an afterlife, no heaven and no hell: no consequences for their hedonistic lifestyle.

Still, she did admire them. Her brothers were so intelligent and talented. She had done her best to preserve all she could of their knowledge: a vast knowledge they either invented or perfected in the sciences, metalworking, agriculture, and music. She even asked them to send tutors for her boys to teach them these valuable skills.

Noah did not allow their children to attend public school in the city. Not only because he didn't want them to hear conflicting religious theories and amoral philosophies, but he wanted to spare them the inevitable teasing and taunting because they were crazy Noah's children. Fortunately, Naamah was fully capable of teaching them the basics of reading, composition and math. Noah often interwove lessons as he worked with his sons, teaching them practical building skills along with important knowledge about their family history, the nature of God, and how God expected them to live.

Life had been good for Naamah the past one hundred years raising the children and helping to furnish the Ark. Settling in a bit more comfortably in their big soft feather bed, she sighed as she wondered why God chose such a violent way to discipline the earth's inhabitants. Not only man and the animals, but also the earth as she knew it, was destroyed.

She knew that the landscape was even now being changed forever. Sometimes the Ark would be rocked as a new fiery mountain erupted through the water throwing glowing hot lava and rocks great distances. The resultant waves would be so large it seemed that the Ark would be capsized, but she knew it wouldn't. Over the decades of her life of waiting, she learned to trust God and knew He would fulfill His promises.

Chapter 10
The Ark, 2348 BC

Japheth sat cross-legged on the deck sketching the image of an oak tree. He saw Shem's shadow approaching just before he heard one of his customary derogatory remarks about the value of his artwork.

"Jay, we really need to conserve our limited supply of paper. You seem to be going through it rather rapidly."

"Shem, what could be more important than preserving, at least on paper, the lost plants and trees that our children may never see?"

"Well, how about the Holy Records as written by our father Adam, not to mention the creation account told to Adam directly from the Creator. Don't you think those are just a little bit more important?"

Japheth really didn't think so, but he decided not to upset his brother. "Those are well preserved on tablets, but pictures of living things are better represented on paper."

He paused and continued to draw some more before he went on, "While I have you here and we have a little time to talk, maybe you can answer some questions, since you seem to be so close to Jehovah's thoughts."

Japheth gathered up his charcoal and paper. "Why was the Flood necessary? I know that the world was evil, but why didn't God just destroy the wicked people and the violent giants and leave the innocent plants and animals alone to live out their natural lives?" Japheth couldn't help the tone of antagonism in his question; he was overwhelmed by the apparent cruelty of God.

Shem sighed and started to walk away, but turned back. "Japheth, I am weary of trying to explain the supremacy of God to you. Why don't you get it? We, as created humans are only a poor reflection of the Creator God. We were made to love and worship Him and to receive love and blessings from Him. He desires our friendship, but demands our trust. We are not capable of understanding God's actions. We cannot even begin to comprehend His holiness."

"Shem, I've heard all that before, and it still doesn't answer my question. Why did God take the lives of the innocent along with the wicked?"

Shem looked at him quizzically, "Innocents? What innocents? You know that God told our father that the only righteous humans left on the earth were our parents, so what 'innocents' are you talking about?"

"The children, but then I suppose they would eventually follow in their parents' footsteps, but what about the animals not on the Ark and …"

Shem interrupted him, "Japheth, let me give you some brotherly advice. Spend more time in prayer and less time drawing trees. When you approach God with a pliable spirit rather than a rebellious one, your questions will more likely be answered. These are not just how and why questions like we learned to answer in school, but are basic spiritual issues that require faith, a faith in God who has all the answers and a faith to accept the answer when it is given to you. God is God, He is not obligated to inform us of His decisions nor does He need our approval of His actions."

Japheth still wasn't convinced, but he was tired of Shem's preaching. He thanked him and let the subject drop. Shem turned away and appeared to be preoccupied with some other matter. Jay felt a tear welling up and starting to fall from his eye. He wiped it off before it made a spot on his artwork.

"Get a grip Jay, it's a tree. I'll see you later, I've work to do," He walked away, shaking his head.

Japheth let his mind wander back to the dense lush forest near their former farm. He closed his eyes and could imagine sitting under one of those old trees, one of the giant oaks that had existed since the creation, over one thousand years ago. He closed his eyes and again felt their power. In his mind, he enjoyed the memory of the strength and warmth of the branches, almost as a surrounding embrace. Even the roots seemed to reach out and up to nourish his spirit as he sat reverently under the gigantic oaks in the forest, escaping momentarily the drudgery of the Ark's construction.

Jay wondered if he would live long enough to experience that comforting feeling again. The trees epitomized power and immortality then, now God had destroyed them all. Another set of tears started to well up, but he quickly stopped his mourning as he suddenly remembered he told Cassie he would help her gather eggs and clean the nesting boxes. Jay quickly finished storing away his artwork and rushed off to find her.

***

Cassia, or Cassie as her husband called her, didn't really need Japheth to help her. Gathering eggs, removing the old bedding, and then putting clean straw into the nesting boxes wasn't a difficult task. She had asked him to help just because she liked to spend time with him. She was placing the eggs in a pliable woven reed basket, the handle draped over her shoulder leaving both hands available for her work, when Japheth appeared.

"Jay, how can some of your family eat these precious things when they know they would have grown up to be cute little chicks?"

"If someone didn't eat them the whole Ark would be overrun with chickens. Three eggs a day would make a lot of little chicks, not to mention the eggs from the other poultry and all the wild birds."

Cassie thought that would be wonderful, an Ark even more full of birds. Besides, she knew that if they left the eggs with the hens they would quit laying and sit on their nests, but she didn't want to argue the point.

"Well, at least they do feed them to some of the other animals. The animals don't realize that is just a form of infanticide, but we do."

Cassie stopped and smiled at him. She wanted to talk about more pleasant things, not put him on the defensive over his family's eating habits. She changed the subject and put down her basket to give him an affectionate hug.

"I am so glad you are my husband, I don't know what I'd do without you." Cassie briefly thought about what life would be like if she had married one of his brothers and laughed out loud.

"What's so funny?"

"I was thinking how incompatible I would be with either of your brothers, self-righteous Shem or fun-loving Ham. I wouldn't be able to stand being married to either one of them."

Japheth smiled, "Don't worry, Honey, I don't think they could stand you either. You're too free spirited for Shem's rigid theology, and Ham would get bored with your love of animals."

He pulled back from her embrace and asked, "Are you almost done? I'm getting hungry. It must be time for dinner."

Cassie was more than a little disappointed that their romantic interlude in the chicken pen was so short and not the time of emotional intimacy she had planned. She missed him during the day and longed for his gentle touch when they were apart. Cassie sighed but smiled at him and said teasingly "I wanted to spend some valuable alone-time with you and you can only think about dinner?"

Jay sheepishly smiled at her and kissed her forehead. He picked up her basket with his left hand and tenderly reached for her hand with his right and led her out of the pen. Cassie awkwardly secured the door with her one free hand, not wanting to let go of Jay. They slowly made their way to the dining room in light-hearted enjoyment of each other.

During dinner it happened again: the nagging feeling that she knew Zalith, or at least had seen her somewhere before, kept haunting Cassia. She just couldn't place her, but she knew somewhere in the recent past their paths had crossed. That in itself was strange, Cassia knew very few people outside of her family and the farm workers. She seldom went to Tymorrah; she found it repulsive: especially the smell of the daily burning of the sacrifices, innocent animals offered to the gods of the city. That was her objection to all the organized religions. Even Noah's God demanded sacrifices of innocent blood for Him to forgive sins. She just couldn't understand how the shedding of innocent blood could help to appease any god, let alone a God that was supposed to be the Creator of them all, humans and animals. What could be its meaning? Surely, an all-powerful Creator-God didn't need any such assistance from his lowly creations.

The sacrifices to the idols of Tymorrah at least made a little more sense. They were necessary for the god's sustenance. Her father, a religious skeptic, had often laughed over the uselessness of a god that needed to be fed. He would entertain the family with irreverent jokes about the town's religious practices. "Why didn't they just make gods that weren't so hungry?" he would sarcastically ask as he smoked his after-dinner pipe. The family joined in the laughter and her father seemed very pleased with himself.

Although her father didn't respect their religion, he didn't mind making a profit by selling them pounds and pounds of "pharmacologically useful" agricultural products.

Cassie forced herself to stop thinking about religion and concentrate on where she had seen Zalith before, but try as she might, she just couldn't place her. *After all, blue-eyed blondes weren't that common. I'll remember sometime.*

***

Later that night Cassia sat straight up in bed and gasped, "The huntress. That was Zalith. That's where I saw her before."

Cassia remembered the day. She stood hidden in the woods, silently observing a magnificent buck in the clearing. Suddenly he lifted his head, sensing some danger. But it was too late. He fell, wailing his once strong legs and struggling to breathe. Blood was pouring out of an arrow wound to his chest.

Cassia saw the band of royal hunters quickly dismount and run to the buck.

"Great shot Princess, right in the heart, " one of them said as the marksman emerged from the woods, still mounted on her prancing horse and carrying her bow. She had a quiver of arrows strapped to her back.

"What should we do with him," one of the other hunters asked.

The princess casually replied, "Just bring the head for a trophy, the meat will taste too 'gamy' ".   She threw back her fur-trimmed leather cloak, revealing a white tiger-skin lining.

Cassia knew only royalty were allowed to wear white tiger skin. She was disgusted, but had to admit the cloak was beautiful. The hunting party quickly beheaded the buck and rode off, leaving Cassia as the only mourner.

She relaxed and snuggled under the covers close to Jay, amazed that he slept through her outburst. *That couldn't have been Zalith; they called her 'Princess'. It must just be someone who resembled her, a distant cousin or something.* She couldn't imagine gentle Zalith engaged in such a cruel pastime, not to mention the physical strength it would take to wield the bow while riding a horse. Everyone knew how weak Zalith was. She couldn't even lift the milk buckets.

At least that mystery is solved and I can quit worrying about where I had seen her before. Still, it is quite a resemblance; the huntress even had the same triumphant glow that Zalith has when something pleases her.

Chapter 11

Tymorrah, Sunday, December 7th, 2349 BC

Dehlia relaxed for the first time in what felt like years, but was in reality only a few short months. She had spent a lot of time and energy secretly gathering all of the most important spell books, drug formulations, idols, candles, robes, hats, star charts, and magic tricks for Zalith. Then she secretly smuggled them to her daughter, now married to the Preacher's son and difficult to contact these days. She was able to rest now since Noah and his family had entered their boat and had not emerged for about a week, so nothing else could be brought to Zalith. Still, she had been busy, covering her tracks and trying to explain to her husband why Zalith was off visiting her cousins for so long. Something had better happen soon or she was going to raid that boat and take her daughter back from those ridiculous people.

She was beginning to doubt her decision to link Zalith with that crackpot. Maybe she had just been taken in by Noah's sense of urgency that day when they were shopping in the city. But on the other hand, all her instincts, all her spiritual contacts, even her star charts, told her she was right; a disaster was coming.

All the secrecy and lying to everyone, even her husband, was amusing, but exhausting. She had to be very careful not to let anyone know she gave any credence to Noah's preaching. Her standing as Head Priestess would surely suffer. *Well, I suppose that is unimportant now, but what if the world continues as it is, and Noah's shown to be the fool that everyone else thinks he is?* At least no one thought that it was unusual for Zalith to be visiting her cousins. Such a trip was common for a young lady of Zalith's age, who then returned home and married; but Dehlia couldn't keep up that charade for much longer.

She lied to her palace guards, not because she cared what they thought, but she knew rumors would start in the barracks and she wanted to control what information leaked to the outside. She needed the guards' strength to move all of Zalith's religious equipment, not to mention her large wardrobe. When asking for their promise of secrecy, she knew it wouldn't take long for the gossip to spread from the barracks. She didn't want that gossip to include any hint of a royal family member believing in Noah's prophecies. When they met Zalith in the woods near what they called 'the lunatic's house', they were not surprised. The elite guards were told from the very beginning of Zalith's relationship with Ham that she was on a secret undercover mission to discover Noah's real motives.

Dehlia explained to them she had some inside information, that maybe Noah wasn't just crazy, but was planning a rebellion. The Flood story was just his attempt at a smoke screen and the big boat was actually a secret fortress. The whole rebellion was being planned under the cover of religious fanaticism. She knew her story sounded pretty contrived, but palace guards were employed for their strength and loyalty, not their reasoning abilities. She knew she could order them to do anything, even to harm their own family, and they would obey her without question. *I'll have to do that someday, just for fun, to see what happens.* She dozed off trying to decide which guard's loyalty she would test first.

Dehlia awoke to a strange sound; it was as if someone was throwing pebbles at the palace. She angrily thought that whoever was doing such a thing might just be asking to be the next public sacrifice. She called for one of her servants to go see what was happening, but no one responded. *What was going on?* She wasn't accustomed to being ignored.

Quite exasperated, she finally got up to investigate. When she pulled back the drapes and looked out her bedroom window, she discovered it wasn't pebbles hitting the roof, but drops of water. Her relieved but apprehensive laughter filled the room, but no one else was in the palace to hear her. They had all rushed outside to see this new phenomenon. Water falling from the sky! Just as Noah predicted! Dehlia watched as the population of the city poured into the streets and courtyards to experience this new wonder. Everyone was joyfully dancing and playing like children as the gentle drops hit their faces and splashed off the cobblestones onto their feet. Many took off their shoes and stomped in the newly formed puddles.

The soft raindrops soon turned into sheets of water, as the entire sky became an angry giant waterfall. People began to panic and run for cover. Some slipped on the wet street and were trampled by the others who were wildly looking for shelter. Roofs collapsed. The streets rapidly filled with water. The rain was coming down so fast and hard that soon Dehlia couldn't see very well, but she could hear the waning of the bleating of farm animals as they floated past her window, caught in the current of the river that was once the street. She wondered when the water would reach her third-story bedroom; or perhaps the roof would collapse first, crushing her and sending her tumbling down to the raging torrent.

She didn't doubt the destruction of the earth, it would happen as Noah foretold. She didn't fear death. She knew her faithful life, as the priestess of Inanna would bring her great honor in the afterlife: but she wanted to be in control of the situation. She didn't want to wait, yielding her fate to Noah and his God. Drowning was a terrible way to die. She would proudly choose her own method, if not her own time to die. She rumbled through her drawer looking for her cache of hidden hemlock.

Suicide at this particular moment wasn't the reason she had obtained and hidden it, she really didn't think much about death until recently. She bought the hemlock to use on others. Her husband was becoming too infatuated with one of the younger wives, Tilmah. Her plan was to poison both of them, and then she would reign with one of her sons, who of course would be married to Zalith. *So much for that plan*, she thought as she found the hemlock wrapped in one of her silk dresses. She mixed the potion in her water glass and quickly drank it.

She heard a noise in the hallway and turned to see who had finally thought about her welfare. It was her husband, but *she* wasn't his concern, he had knocked over a table in his haste to help Tilmah. She guessed they were probably heading for the royal yacht, used for river parades and sport fishing. She laughed at their dilemma, imagining everyone else was thinking the same thing. *There would be great hordes of people, pouring onto the yacht and the other fishing vessels, thinking they could escape the deluge. How silly! The boats would already be full of water, and the extra hundreds of passengers would capsize or just sink the vessels altogether.*

Dehlia was really feeling the effects of the poison now. She happily relaxed as her spirit lifted from her body. She was floating now, rising above her lifeless body, motionless on the bed. She saw the palace collapse and become more debris in the newly formed river. But she was safe above the doomed earth now and nothing seemed very important. She heard music beautiful beyond description and saw swirling colors she had never before imagined. Dehlia was becoming more and more a part of the swirling ribbons of vaporous colors. She began to see beautiful, benevolent smiling faces, faces welcoming her to the afterlife. Dehlia was delighted; she had never felt such peace and comfort.

Everything changed. Luminous colors darkened. Smiling faces became mocking and unbearably ugly. Dehlia began to feel as if she were falling, uncontrollably falling. Accustomed to being in control, now she could do nothing to prevent her descent, nor did she know what was ahead of her. The air became bitter cold, so cold she felt as if she were burning. The falling stopped, jarred to a halt as she landed on a solid but slimy and repulsive surface. She was in total darkness. An unbearable stench filled the air, pierced with evil-toned screeching.

***

Dehlia never believed in hell. In her view, it was an imaginary place used to threaten people into obeying those ridiculously binding laws of the Jehovah worshippers. Was this it? Was this hell? She had no idea how much time had passed. Each painful moment seemed an eternity. The primary figure, the one who seemed to be in charge, spent a lot of his time with her, personally making sure of her misery. Periods of light interrupted the darkness, making his presence known.

Dehlia didn't understand how she could feel pain; she had seen her body back in her palace bedroom. Wasn't she totally in the spirit? Weren't physical sensations impossible? She once believed that after death all knowledge would be given her. Now she only had more questions, horrible nagging questions. For one who had been used to the absolute control of her life and those around her, the absence of choice was unbearable. She was in total subjection, one moment being tormented by screeching bird-like creatures, with the sensation of sharp beaks tearing the flesh from her bones, to the next moment in the court of the Ruler being mocked and ridiculed by hoards of bony demons with ugly, twisted asymmetrical faces. The Ruler seemed to get a great deal of pleasure from her total humiliation.

Thankfully, just when she had despaired of any relief, a cloud of light surrounded her. A magnificent creature was before her, awaiting her worship. She knew instantly who he was. "Lucifer, my Lord", she reverently proclaimed as she bowed down first to her knees and then further with her face and hands on the floor.

"Thank you, my Great One, for saving me."

"My daughter, you will be bound here until the final defeat of our enemy, Jehovah and his angels. You must be patient."

"My Lord, please let me go to my daughter, Zalith, to warn her: to tell her that we have been deceived, everything in my life was a deception."

"Dehlia, I am not without compassion. You will be allowed a short visit, but you must not let anyone else know of your presence. Prepare yourself and I will transport you to Zalith."

Dehlia, still bowing, closed her eyes and waited. Not wanting to seem impatient, she waited longer. She could contain herself no more, "My Lord, you said that I could visit my daughter and warn her."

"I lied." She held her hands over her ears to soften the penetrating evil laughter. The light faded as the beautiful Lucifer transformed into the dark and hideous Ruler.

"Do you think she would listen? Besides, I have my own plans for Zalith, and I don't need you to interfere." He disappeared and Dehlia was enveloped in a heat that she desperately hoped would burn her into total annihilation, but only left her tortured and consumed with an unquenched thirst. She longed for just one drop of the water she had seen flooding the earth as she died. She cried out to the Ruler,

"Please! Just give me one drop of water to moisten my parched tongue. Please!"

Distant cruel laughter was her answer.

Chapter 12

The Ark, 2348 BC

Zalith searched cautiously in the reptile room on a rare venture into the animal quarters. A gentle but persistent voice had led her there. She wondered if her Mother was going to contact her here. *Surely not, she always hated snakes.* The snakes and lizards were all in a supernatural, semi-sleepy state that enabled the crew of the Ark to care for them more easily. *Was their hibernation really Jehovah's doing, as Noah said? Probably not: her Earth Mother may just be protecting her. Were the gods working in concert: the gentle goddess and the jealous god? Oh well, doesn't matter, the results are the same.* While hibernating, their growth was slowed almost to a stop. Zalith was relieved; she didn't want to have to deal with a rapidly growing dragon, even though she was confident her goddess would protect her. Her mission was too important.

She couldn't help admiring the brightly colored snakes. *Did they really walk upright in Eden? Did Jehovah really remove their legs? Does He even have that ability? Wasn't it another creation story used to explain a natural occurrence to the uninitiated?* Although these questions crossed her mind, she didn't dwell on them. She knew all knowledge would be available to her eventually.

Suddenly, one of the snakes raised its head from its dormant coiled position and began speaking to her in a familiar voice, "Zalith"

"Mother! I knew you would contact me soon! Have you been re-incarnated as a snake? Are you being punished?"

"Don't be ridiculous, dear. I just thought it would be a good joke to come to you in the same form that Lucifer came to Mother Eve, when he showed her how to become a goddess. But listen, you have an important job to do."

"Good. Things are getting pretty boring around here."

"Remember in the Garden, how Jehovah promised that he would send a Redeemer, from the seed of Eve. Of course He called Him a Redeemer, but His real purpose is to destroy us and our kind, Eve's pure legacy. You need to prevent His appearance."

"But Mother, how can I prevent the Redeemer from coming?"

"Simple, my dear. You just have to prevent his birth."

"But, Mother, from this side of eternity that is not so clearly seen. Who is he and when is he to be born?"

"Well, my dear, He most likely won't appear for a while, but he has to have parents. You are in a unique position to thwart his appearance from the beginning. You and Ham don't need any royal rivals; you can prevent a multi-millennial conflict between His seed and yours by preventing the birth of His ancestor. Think of it as a peace mission."

"But I still don't know whose birth I am preventing."

"Isn't it obvious? Shem's son is the logical choice. Shem is the only one of Noah's sons who truly follows Jehovah, our enemy. Naamah is past childbearing, and Japheth and Cassia are ineffective fence sitters. They don't know whom to follow. Forget them, we will deal with those two later. Debra must be the one chosen to be the Redeemer's mother. Prevent Debra from conceiving by Shem and you will have succeeded. Bye, I have to go. Our Angel of Light needs me for another errand."

Satan left the snake and it collapsed back into its coils.

Zalith began to plan as she walked back to her room. *Sounds easy enough. There must be a thousand ways to prevent Debra from conceiving. I could kill one of them, but it would have to look like an accident or maybe even suicide. Anyway, that would leave a lot more work for Ham, and I might even be forced into helping. I could make Shem fall in love with me and Ham would kill him in a jealous rage. But that still reduces our manpower too much, who would build my palace and my temple? I'll think of something.*

Most men can be controlled easier than women, with or without actually having sex with them. A little flattery and flirting can go a long way. But then, perhaps I could bring Debra into the secret sisterhood. At times I am lonely, and a confidant would be nice. Surely Shem wouldn't stay with an open goddess worshipper. But it might take too long to convert her. Besides, even with two goddess worshippers, the others might try to harm us in a self-righteous rage. Better to be as secretive as possible. Hmm…Noah might lift the ban on sex any time now. I'll have to think of something else, probably an affair with Shem. I'll make sure Debra finds out, then she will feel betrayed and hate him, perhaps she will even be suicidal. If that doesn't work, Debra might have to have an accident. I suppose if she does get pregnant, I could always slip her the potion of ergot and clover that will make her miscarry. But as mother always said, prevention is the best cure.

Chapter 13

The Ark, 2348 BC

Shem woke up in a cold sweat. Not that dream again: Zalith. Shem considered himself a model husband, totally devoted to and in love with Debra. Then why was he dreaming about his brother's wife? He hadn't planned on this. During the day, he pushed any sexual thoughts away from his mind. He kept busy, and that was certainly easy enough to do: there was never any lack of work on the Ark.

But at night, visions of Zalith filled his dreams: romantic visions, erotic visions. Nothing like this had ever happened to him before. He had always been proud of the control he thought he had over his emotions and desires. He would never do anything to hurt Debra, or Ham. *Zalith doesn't know what she does to me. Like last night after devotions, she sought me out. She wanted to ask a spiritual question of a rather personal nature; she leaned close so only I could hear. How could I think with her so close? Why did she ask me if sexual fantasies about men were wrong? Why didn't she ask my mother? I suppose it's because she considers me as an older role model, beyond such temptations. Little does she know. Or does she know? Sometimes I feel she is trying to attract me, maybe even seduce me. No. I won't allow my desires to cloud my perceptions of her character.*

If she is attracted to me, it isn't in a sexual way. She's the only other one, besides my parents, that seem even remotely interested in the weekly scripture studies. Even Debra is bored and distracted. The others try to pay attention, but their hearts aren't in it. They daydream, or even sometimes doze off. Zalith hangs on my every word, asking questions and making pertinent observations. Ham is totally detached from spiritual matters. That's Zalith's attraction to me, I'm sure of it. She is eager for instruction. Coming from a family of non-believers, the study of God and his attributes are new to her. She yearns for spiritual growth, and Ham isn't able to help her. He's in desperate need of spiritual growth himself. There's nothing of a sexual interest on her part, I'm sure. It's only my imagination. I should be ashamed of myself! This is all Dad's fault. The ban on sex is unnatural and leads my body and mind to seek other means of gratification. Maybe that's the whole problem. If I fantasized about Debra, I would not be able to resist the temptation to act out those fantasies, her being so close, right beside me. I could never act on any fantasies about Zalith; she is safely unattainable. I am going to talk to Dad tomorrow. Maybe it's time to lift the ban.

***

Debra hoped she didn't hear what she thought she heard. *Did Shem call out Zalith's name in his sleep?*

Chapter 14

The Ark, 2348 BC

Cassia looked fondly at her intricate silver pipe. It was wonderfully crafted, with inlays of mother of pearl and tiny precious gems completing the miniature hummingbird on the side. *How was this made? Obviously, fashioned by a very skilled workman. He probably used a mold for the main body, no, wait, two molds. I can just barely see the seam, and then perhaps the hummingbird was made separately and attached later, as well as the ivory hand rest and mouthpiece that kept the user from the heat of the silver. Yes, there is a seam there too; I can see it when I turn the pipe just right. I wonder how long it took to make it? Hours, I'm sure, lots of hours. There were hundreds of these pipes for sale in the shops of Tymorrah; just those pipes must have taken many days of skilled craftsmanship, let alone the time it took to make all the other marvelously manufactured items in the uncounted shops in the city.*

She suddenly felt dizzy as she realized the finality of the destruction, the loss of all of the artwork and the beautifully crafted objects. *Everything!* She gripped her wooden dresser to prevent herself from falling. *I was so busy mourning the loss of the animals and the forests, I hadn't thought of anything else. The magnificent buildings, the elaborate temples with their inlaid tiles and frescoed walls: lost. The gold and silver jewelry, the pottery and statues, the intricate tapestries: destroyed. How can they be replaced?*

"They can't!" she gasped out loud and sat on the bed with her pipe in her hands. A heavy sadness came over her and her eyes filled with tears. *Maybe we can rebuild. I know Jay, his father and his brothers have a lot of building skills, they're all skillful and well educated, but four men can't build a palace or a library. Library! All the books, the histories, the sciences, the literature, they're lost, too*! She was openly weeping now.

"Cassie! Why did you even bring that thing? You promised me." Japheth sat down beside her. Cassie could feel his anger as he looked at the pipe, but felt him soften when he noticed her tears.

"What is it Honey? Thinking about your family again?" He tenderly took her in his arms try to comfort her.

"Jay, our children will never..."

"Yes, yes we will have children soon." He gently pulled her head to his chest and wrapped his hands around her curly red hair. "Don't be so sad, I can't stand to see you this way."

Her tears began to subside and she smiled at him. "I have you, and that's all I need."

"Cassie, you didn't bring anything to smoke in that, did you?" Japheth said as he looked at the pipe in her lap.

"No, Japheth. I brought it because it's the only thing I have left of my family. Remember, my parents gave it to me on my eighteenth birthday."

"That's good. We have enough to deal with, Debra's drinking and all. Are you better now? I really should get back to work, I just wanted to see you for a little while."

"Yes, you always make me feel better." He left and she thought, how *true: even though he totally misunderstood my reason for being so upset, he did make me feel better. Well, sometimes I do wish that I brought something to smoke. Not peyote, too radical, but some marijuana wouldn't be so bad. But I promised Jay, so it is a good thing I don't have any to tempt me.*

She again looked at her delicate pipe and thought about her family. *No wonder Jay thought I was thinking about them. It was so horrible!* She remembered that awful day started out fine, even more than fine. The sky was beautifully blue, the grass a bright emerald green and the dusky woods comfortably cool and shady. She had taken her pipe and the special mix her father made for her on her daily woodland adventure. He told her not to smoke it alone, because sometimes people had bad reactions, tried to hurt themselves or others. But he felt that the chance for a mind-expanding experience for her was worth the risk. No matter what, the effect would wear off eventually, he told her. She didn't heed his warning. She liked being alone. She relaxed and curled up in her special place in the woods: a nest-like, curled tree branch, high enough to feel hidden in the leaves, and big enough that she could relax and not worry about falling.

As she lit her pipe that day, she wished that her friend Japheth were there. He didn't like drugs though, so probably just as well he wasn't. He especially didn't like this type of drug, one that people used to get in touch with spirits. She didn't know if she even believed in spirits, although sometimes it seemed to her as if the whole forest was full of them; *It can't just be the drugs making me imagine things. My father does drugs, especially this kind, all the time and he doesn't believe in spirits.* He jeeringly told her that sometimes his customers revealed to him that when they used this mix, their spirits actually left their bodies. Sometimes, his clients said, their spirits became transformed into animals or somehow combined with an animal's spirit. More than one of his customers claimed this mix would take them on a personal spiritual journey, gaining insights they would never have had otherwise. Other customers said their disembodied spirits just traveled to distant places, wonderful places, she imagined as her father was talking. Of course her father didn't believe them. He didn't think any of these things actually happened, he thought their minds were only playing tricks on them, The drugs allowing them to experience strange images and sensations. Nevertheless, he took their money and laughed at their religion after they left with their parcels.

Cassie hoped she would be able to have at least a little bit of a spiritual experience, maybe even one of those animal possessions. That would be such an adventure! She was staring at her arm, covered in buckskin. She didn't really approve of killing animals for their skin, or for any reason. But *she* didn't kill it, and the leather was so soft and enveloping. Her mother made it especially for her to protect her in her forest wanderings. She wore the buckskin respectfully, as a tribute to its previous owner. It helped her blend into the woods, camouflaging her. Many times she had remained undetected by roving bands of hoodlums, so common lately. She would hear them coming for miles; they were so loud, so out of place in the forest.

Once she had seen a murder, below this very tree branch. She smoked her pipe and remembered that horrible incident. A band of thieves was drinking, laughing and shoving each other through the forest. Then the laughter stopped as one of the men pushed another one, this time in anger. The two men started fighting. She winced as she heard the hammering blows. The one who appeared to be the elder pulled a knife and stabbed the younger man in the chest. His collapsing lungs let out a muffled scream as he hit the ground. The pierced heart pumped and spurted blood until his body was lifeless. His companions just laughed and left him there. She began to climb down as their voices faded in the distance.

She became motionless halfway down the tree. Their voices were becoming louder again so she reasoned they must be facing her and any movement she made might be detected. She clung to the tree trunk and hoped they wouldn't look up. *Did they know she was there? Was that the reason for their return?*

"That was dumb – leaving your knife. And we should take his money and jewelry, too"

"We! Why should you get any? I killed him."

"Because I am going to corroborate your story of how we were attacked. He was the boss's brother; and the boss is going to demand an explanation or our lives. In fact, maybe we should just take the money; his jewelry can be identified."

"Who cares? We'll just hide it and sell it later."

Cassie's arms and legs were killing her. *Were they going to stay there forever?*

After robbing the body and retrieving the knife, they finally left. Cassie climbed back into her tree branch nest to recuperate and make sure they were really gone this time. She briefly thought about contacting the authorities and report what she had seen. *Not a good idea. Witnesses to a gang murder had a very short life.*

She inhaled deeply, letting the smoke erase the gruesome memory.

Then it happened. Her buckskin sleeve became warm and even more pliable. Veins and arteries appeared. Was this in her altered imagination or was it really happening? She couldn't tell. Normal perceptions were gone. Suddenly she was on the ground, landing on all four feet. Four feet! Or rather hooves, she marveled. She tossed her new long neck, and started to run, not running away from anything or toward anything, just running for the sheer joy of it. She reveled in her own strength, the muscles of her limbs carrying her body effortlessly across the ground. With every passing moment, she became more deer and less human. Soon she came upon a grazing herd in a meadow, the yearlings running and jumping. She joined in tossing her head and play-fighting with the other young deer. At first the yearlings were cautious but soon accepted her. After playing relentlessly for hours, she was getting tired. She needed a nap desperately. She curled up in a nicely protected area at the edge of the meadow.

***

Cassia remembered waking to a strange smell in her newly sensitive nostrils. In the distance, she could hear the roar of one of those terrible dragons. All the 'other' deer heard it too and rapidly disappeared. *What was that smell?* She stretched out her slim but powerful front leg, but it was her arm again. Her hand felt strange to her, she moved it, but she wasn't really sure she was feeling it. Slowly her senses returned and she was able to stand.

Her mind was coming back to reality. *Fire!* She looked towards home. *Smoke. Maybe the workers were just burning debris off the fields, but this wasn't the season for that. The crops had not yet been harvested.* She was running now, and wished she still had the speed she had experienced earlier. *Was it real? Was it a dream? Why did I wake up in the forest if it wasn't real?* Dread rapidly replaced her peaceful dreamlike afternoon experience. *Something is wrong; I need to get back home.*

Dusk was falling as she approached the clearing of her family's farm. The fields were burning; strange horsemen were looting and destroying everything in their path. She saw her father near the gate. She wanted to run to him, but instinctively remained hidden from the view of the raiders. *Who or what was he talking to? That must be one of the Nephilim.* She had heard horrible stories about them. This man was absolutely huge and riding on an even more humongous lizard, the kind they called dragons. *But how could that be? No mere human could control one of those beasts*!

At first her father was talking calmly with him, then arguing.

"Is he insane?" she gasped and quickly covered her mouth with her hands. She didn't know exactly what was going on, but she was sure she didn't want those monsters to detect her. Her father had money in his hand. *He must be trying to buy him off.* He had been warned not to antagonize the Nephilim now that they had become rival producers. His friends warned him, they said it was better to go back to raising vegetables than incur their wrath. Her mother had tried to convince him not to deal with these giants, that they were rumored to be the children of demons and pure evil.

"Don't be ridiculous", he told her, "There are no demons. They are simply large humans: nothing more, nothing less. And I can reason with humans. If not, they can be bribed. After all, they are businessmen, just like me."

The Nephilim took the money from her father and sneeringly turned away. Cassia was relieved and started to run home, but when her father turned his back, the horrible creature quickly returned his giant reptile to the gate. In seconds, the giant was again on his way. The headless corpse of her father stood eerily for what seemed an eternity before it fell.

The giant was laughing. He called to his band, "Take the harvest and burn the rest. Leave no one alive, except a maiden or two for your pleasure."

Cassia stood in the shadows in shock. She observed helplessly as the fields and buildings burned. She watched horrified as the horsemen carried off her sisters and some of the younger female workers. She wanted to scream at them, to say something to make them stop, but she knew drawing any attention in her direction would only bring about her capture and demise as well.

She ran back to the forest, looking for a place to hide. She climbed a tree. *They probably won't look up, even if someone did see me.* She amazed herself at being able to reason. *Of course if they find me, I will be trapped, but if they see me on the ground, I wouldn't have a chance. My sisters are so pretty; I hope their beauty saves their lives. Or do I? What kind of horrible life is ahead of them?*

Ashes were falling all around her, tears making two clean tracks down her face. The fire lasted for what seemed like days, but she knew it was only hours. Thankfully, the wind caused by the heat of the fire was blowing away from her and the forest. The raiders were gone now. Most likely they didn't know about her, since they didn't seem to be looking for her. She supposed that they were too busy dividing and selling her family's valuables. She tried to snort out the smell of the burning crops from her nostrils. *They're probably too high to think anyway, indulging all night in stolen mind altering substances.*

She desperately wished she had been home earlier; maybe she could have intervened. Maybe she could have insisted that her family escape into the trees as she did, and not try to reason with such criminals. She didn't know what she was feeling. Perhaps it would have been better if she had died as well. *Where can I go? No one will take me in. They will be afraid of the Nephilim, afraid that I'll make them a target of their ruthlessness.*

She really wanted to escape back into the deer's body. She ran to her special tree, but only the pipe was there, the bag of her mind-altering mix was gone, probably pulled away by some bird, or picked up by some chimpanzee. She smiled as she wondered if the animal that took her drugs was having a human possession experience, and then she was immediately ashamed that she could find humor in anything after what happened.

Japheth! He will help me. Maybe his fanatic family will take me in! She ran desperately toward his house. Then she saw him; he was running just as desperately towards what was left of her house.   She ran after him, calling his name.

Japheth stopped when he saw the devastated farm. Cassie could see him standing and staring, but when she got close enough for him to hear her smoke-damaged voice, he started to run towards the ruins again

"Cassie! Cassie!" He was calling, but she couldn't yell out loudly enough for him to hear her response.

She heard his voice trail off and saw him collapse to his knees, his face in his hands. He was crying out her name between sobs now. They were cries of mourning; any traces of hopeful expectation of her answering him were gone from his voice.

Cassie finally reached the edge of the clearing. Out of breath and her lungs burning from exhaustion and the smoke, she had to wait a little while before she could call out to him. She wasn't going to take one step closer. She didn't want to see what was left of her family; she would rather remember them alive.

"Jay! I'm all right. I'm over here." It seemed as if he were instantly beside her, engulfing her in a tight embrace.

"Cassie, I thought I lost you!" She couldn't answer; only lay crying against his chest.

"When the delivery man told me your father's farm was destroyed and the Nephilim were bragging they left no one alive, my heart literally sank. Cassie, I don't want to live without you, I love you. Marry me. Please marry me."

Chapter 15
The Ark, 2348 BC

After comforting Cassie, Japheth once again retuned to his animal duties. He also thought about the day Cassie lost her family. That was the day he knew he didn't want to live without her. He remembered how they met in the forest. Was it accidental? Did God ordain it? Cassia said maybe the Great Spirit of the forest itself brought them together. He was a little surprised when she said that, but realized that at that time she didn't really know any other way to express a supernatural influence.

Japheth was in the woods the day they met, taking in its deep living richness when he spotted her across the meadow. At first he thought she was an apparition, she looked like a wood nymph from a fairy tale. He silently circled around the edge of the meadow and suddenly stepped out in front of her. Jay saw the terror in her eyes, as she tried to run from him. He gently but firmly grabbed her arm above the elbow and told her not to be afraid, that he had no intention of hurting her.

"Why should I believe you? Let go of me!"

"Shhh… Don't you hear them? Don't let them know we are here. We'll both be killed"

Cassie stopped struggling and then she too heard the bandits approaching.

"C'mon lets climb up this tree. They are on horseback and we don't have time to run. You have a choice, them or me."

Japath knew she was choosing what she thought was the lesser of two evils as he tried to help her climb. She brushed off his hand and scurried up the giant oak with him close behind. They watched the band noisily pass through the meadow and pick up the path on the far side.

After the band left, Japheth again reassured her that he meant her no harm and that she was free to go if she wished. She stayed.

She fascinated him. She was so very different from any other woman he had ever met: no jewelry, no perfume, and no flowing but revealing dress. He convinced her to meet him again. They became friends, but secret friends. He didn't think that his parents would approve of a tree climbing, drug using, spirit-revering female friend.

Once he had asked her if he could call on her at home. She looked embarrassed and stammeringly told him, "I'm sorry Jay. I can't invite you to my house. I can't let my parents know about you."

"But surely once they meet me, they will know I am a safe companion and won't hurt or disrespect you."

"Oh, Jay, that's not it! I am afraid they will disrespect you- make fun of you and your religion and your father and his boat and me too, for associating with you. My Dad and brothers will tease me terribly. I just don't want to deal with it."

Japheth couldn't help falling in love with her. Despite her pagan beliefs, she had a wonderful innocence and a sweet and unpresumptuous way about her. He even loved the confusing way she talked. He loved her never-ending sentences that would have been annoying from anyone else. He was torn. He genuinely loved and respected his parents, but Cassia had an emotional hold on him that was greater than anything he had ever experienced.

He smiled through the dust and sweat on his face as he remembered that Noah and Naamah rather reluctantly agreed to the wedding. Ordinarily, they would have insisted that Cassie go through religious training and be in total agreement with their beliefs, but everyone was so busy with the preparation of the Ark, and these were not normal or ordinary times. They couldn't turn her away, and it didn't seem proper to his parents to allow her to stay there without marriage since she and Jay were obviously romantically involved. The day they made their vows before Methuselah was the happiest day of Jay's life.

Chapter 16

The Ark, 2348 BC

Shem decided to enlist the help of his brothers to try to persuade their father to lift the ban on sex. Japheth readily agreed. Ham told the other two he would go with them, but they should do all the talking.

A few hours before dinner, the three brothers found Noah repairing one of the fishing nets they could now use to gather fresh meat for the carnivores. Japheth began the slightly uncomfortable conversation, "Dad, don't you think you could lift the ban on sex now. Even if our wives would get pregnant immediately, the land will be dry before the child is born."

Noah looked at them patiently and began to speak after he put one more throw into his knot and put down his net. "Look boys, you aren't the ones who would get pregnant. I remember your mother when she was pregnant with each one of you, and it isn't as easy as you three think. Are you willing to do their work, as well as your own, if your wives are not up to performing their duties? Trust me, this boat isn't big enough for three nauseated, tired, grouchy pregnant women. And the food cravings! Your mother would eat the weirdest things. I'm telling you, there isn't enough honey and salt left to keep three pregnant girls happy."

"But Dad, wasn't it worth it? Weren't we worth it? I for one am looking forward to parenthood, and so is Cassie, the sooner the better. "

"Japheth is right. A couple of little ones around here would certainly cheer us all up", Shem decided procreation was a safer argument, since he felt a little uneasy talking so freely with his father about sexual desire.

Shem forced himself to add, "Dad, this is unnatural. It is putting a strain on all of us."

Ham nodded in silent agreement. Shem thought Ham was being cowardly, not having enough backbone to discuss it. Then he suddenly remembered Ham's loss of his first child. *How callous can I be? No wonder he is so silent.*

"Alright boys, let me consider it. I will make an announcement at dinner."

***

After Noah gave the blessing for the food that evening, he asked for everyone's attention. "I have an announcement to make. I am lifting the ban on sexual intercourse."

Shem wondered if his brothers were as excited and relieved as he was. He could barely refrain from shouting and applauding. Noah continued, but Shem wasn't concentrating on his Father's speech.

"But I do want you all to remember that sex does have consequences, consequences that carry large responsibilities. You young ladies need to think very carefully about how a pregnancy and the care of a newborn might complicate your lives. We don't know what the new world will be like. We don't even know when we will be able to disembark. I want all of you to discuss this privately and enter into this phase of your relationship in agreement between both husband and wife."

As Noah was finishing his speech and preparing to eat, his sons hurriedly excused themselves.

With just a hint of amusement, Noah asked, "What's your hurry?"

"We, ..ah ..ah, we have a lot to talk about. You know,.. responsibility and all that" Japheth explained as he took Cassie's hand and pulled her away from the table in mid-bite.

***

Shem quickly forgot about his absent-minded promise to his father to reflect on the possibility of pregnancy and the responsibility that would bring. He had been thinking about Debra all day. Not just sexually, but how much he loved her, how much he missed their intimacy. Tonight wasn't their first time, but it was to be the first time in a long while. He felt nervous. All of his senses seemed heightened; his head was spinning. Debra was taking down her hair. *What was taking her so long?* As she pulled out the last of what seemed to be a million pins, Shem pulled her close. Her hair fell around him as he passionately kissed her neck. He was pleasantly surrounded by the sweet and spicy smell of the lavender and rose perfume emanating from her.

"Debra I've missed the way your hair smells. I've missed everything about you being close to me."

"I've missed you, too. I love you so much", Debra replied from her heart in a soft, deep voice. He tried not to rush things, to make their reunion memorable, but Shem suddenly decided slow lovemaking could wait until tomorrow. He let go of her and urgently started to untie her belt. He was again overwhelmed by how much he loved her and pulled her into another embrace.

"I love you Zalith"

"What!" Debra started beating on his chest and tried to escape from his arms.

"Debra! What's wrong? Was I holding you too tightly? I'm sorry. I will control myself more. Why are you looking at me like that?"

"You Pig! Don't you know? You called me Zalith. I knew you were in love with her. I just didn't want to believe it"

"Debra, I didn't." Shem tried to gently pull her close again.

"Yes you did. Don't you remember which one of us you are with? Do you ever call her Debra?" She said sarcastically as she broke away from him. The antagonism emanating from her body kept him from trying to approach her again. She was gathering up a sheepskin and some blankets.

"Debra, don't leave. It's you I love. I don't know why I said it. I'm not even sure that I did." He grabbed her elbow as she ran past him on the way to find somewhere else to sleep.

"Let go of me!" she demanded. The anger and coldness in her eyes shocked him.

Then she very calmly and deliberately told him, "You are never to touch me again." She began to cry as she ran down the corridor to one of the now empty storage rooms.

What just happened? Calling her the wrong name isn't that big of a problem. Is it? Did I really call her Zalith? Why? Debra is the one I love. Now she hates me. He was surprised as guilt overtook him. *I didn't really do anything wrong, did I? I can't control my dreams At least Debra must really care for me if I can hurt her so easily.* He didn't mean to hurt her. It was Debra with whom he wanted to spend the rest of his life. Debra was the one that he wanted to be the mother of his children. *Why did I call her Zalith?*

He liked to be in control of his actions. It wasn't like him to blurt out something he didn't mean to say. He knew he didn't love Zalith, then why did he use her name in a moment of passion? *If Debra had called me by another man's name, how would I be feeling? I probably wouldn't' even have noticed. Yes I would and I would be pretty jealous and upset, especially if it were one of my brothers – but I wouldn't have assumed she was having an affair. Maybe.*

He picked up his clothes and got ready for bed. Shem decided he needed to do some serious self-evaluation, something he rarely did. Up to this point, situations in his life were pretty much black or white, right or wrong; and decisions had been easy. He had never had to face such a moral dilemma. *I still can't believe I am lusting after my brother's wife.*

Maybe that was it. Maybe I called Debra 'Zalith' out of some twisted need to confess to her. Debra is right. I am a pig.

He prayed to God that he would be able to eventually fix the emotional rift between them. He was drifting off to sleep when the enormity of his actions hit him. For the first time in his life, he realized he was capable of all manner of depravities. *I'm not any better than those that perished. Why doesn't God instantly destroy me now?*

He had seen first-hand God's righteous fury. Shem had always believed God loved him because he was a good man. He worked hard; he didn't lie or steal. But now, for the first time in his life he was facing the fact that he wasn't so good after all. He was beginning to understand the necessity of the sacrifices that God demanded. They weren't for God; God didn't need the blood of bulls for His existence, the blood was a substitution, a symbol of confession and repentance of the one offering the sacrifice. Of course Shem had heard this many times. He even preached it himself. He never thought it really applied to him.

***

Eventually Shem fell into a troubled sleep. In the morning, he sleepily reached out to Debra, but the cold and empty bed jolted him back to reality. He was determined to mend their relationship. *Surely she can't seriously be considering leaving me. It's not like she has anywhere to go or any other prospects for marriage.* He hurriedly got dressed and rushed off to find her. He met Ham in the hall.

"I saw Debra folding blankets in a storage room, sooo…. my guess is she said 'no'." Ham grinned as he told his brother, " I bet there are some lonesome sheep downstairs. Maybe one of them would be your roommate."

Shem was annoyed that Ham couldn't contain his obnoxious laughter. He had a vague momentary feeling that Ham was even a little happy to see that he and Debra were having some marital problems.

"Can't you be serious about anything?" Shem angrily replied. "That wasn't even remotely funny."

"Hey, don't be so huffy! At least my wife isn't sleeping in a storage room."

Shem, exasperated at his brother's amusement over his pain, almost made a remark about Zalith not being as content with Ham as Ham thought she was, but stopped. That wouldn't really help the situation, but the thought crossed his mind that Ham wouldn't find the reason for Debra not sleeping with him as being very funny.

78

"So you saw Debra. Where is she?"

"Second room on the left, in the storage corridor."

Shem hurried past Ham to find her.

"Debra, can I come in?" He respectfully asked her. Shem was doing his best not to be antagonistic. He really did love her and he wanted her back.

"I need to talk to you."

"Stay there. You can talk to me from the doorway. Or better yet, leave" Debra haughtily said.

Shem could tell that she was not in the mood for reconciliation, but decided to ignore that request and begin his speech. "After you left last night, I missed you so much. I didn't mean to hurt you. You don't realize just how much you mean to me. Please come back."

"I don't want to. I would rather live alone. If you weren't you, if you weren't so pious, if you hadn't led me to believe that I was the only one, if you had just admitted to me you were like all the rest, maybe I wouldn't be so upset."

"Debra, that's it. I'm so glad you understand. I think God is using sexual temptation to allow me to grow spiritually."

"Shem! You ...you... you self-righteous obnoxious jerk! How dare you use God as an excuse for your lust! Get out!"

"But Debra, I didn't mean it to sound like that. Besides, we have an obligation to stay together, to re-populate the world."

"Really! Maybe you can go populate it with Zalith. And don't try to make *me* feel guilty. If your all-powerful God wants me to have children, he can make me a new husband."

Shem's pride stopped him from any further begging. "You know where to find me when you come to your senses." He turned and walked away.

He found his mother working in the kitchen. Shem was constantly amazed at her ingenuity. She had devised a stove and vents to the outside, constructed years ago with help from her metalworking brother, Tubal-cain. When they ran out of wood, she had her sons use the fishing nets to bring in driftwood.

Shem ordinarily wouldn't burden her with his personal problems, but he hoped she could talk some sense into Debra. "Mom, could you do me a favor?"

"Sure, if I possibly can, Honey"

Shem thought that he was way too old and mature to be called 'Honey', but he let it drop. "Debra is acting unreasonably. Could you talk to her?"

"All right, but why? What happened?"

"Nothing really. She's being very touchy lately. I can't understand it. She is turning every little thing into a disaster."

"Hmm…maybe it has something to do with her not drinking anymore. Getting over an addiction can cause some emotional upsets. And, Honey, you know women get emotional when it is that time… .. "

"Maybe" Shem interrupted her. He wasn't up to that conversation. Women made that too convenient of an excuse anyway. "We had a fight last night and she moved into one of the storage rooms."

"Oh my, she is upset. I'll talk to her later. Let's give her some time to calm down."

"Thanks, Mom"

***

Debra was working as diligently as she always did, cleaning and raking out the pens: then feeding and watering then watering, feeding, and cleaning some more. It never ended. But her mind was on her personal problems. *Was she losing her sanity? Why didn't she have better control over herself? Why did she say those awful things to Shem? I really do love him; I can forgive him. Eventually. It really wasn't that important. I was just shocked. When he called me Zalith, it was such a surprise that I lost it. I don't believe Shem would actually have an affair with Zalith. Why did I make him think that I thought so? Besides, how could that happen when there isn't much time for anything but work? And no privacy. Not to mention that Ham spends every spare minute with his wife. He waits on her hand and foot. I will go back to Shem. I just need some time. Besides, fighting does add some excitement to life. I like him chasing me, begging me to come back. I will be more receptive the next time he asks me. It will be almost like he is courting me again. He was so sweet to me then. Our reunion will be so romantic!*

Romance. Is that his idea of romance: to call me Zalith? He held me and called me Zalith! She felt like someone punched her in the stomach. *He can wait; maybe wait forever.* She didn't want to, but she started weeping again and slumped down in the goat pen, her back against the wall, with her head in her lap.

80

Chapter 17
Hell, undetermined time

Dehlia's torment was again momentarily disrupted by a personal visit from Lucifer, and she once again fell to her knees to worship him. What did she have to lose? "My Lord, have you seen my daughter? Did she accomplish the mission you gave her?"

The chamber echoed with sarcastic laughter. He finally spoke, "Dehlia, since you are here and can't interfere, let me share something with you, something you will be able to contemplate through the ages. Do you really think that a mere human can interfere with The Most High's promises? Do you think that the prophecies can be altered? Do you think that God would bother to save eight of his precious humans and then let one of them destroy the others? It amuses me to watch them try to thwart God. I do *so* enjoy it when one of you humans becomes trapped by my lies and believes they can alter God's plans: utterly pathetic, but thoroughly entertaining".

"My Lord, I don't know. I know nothing about this God, this Most High."

"Most amusing" He roared at his own joke. "I do make some good puns don't I? I love words. They can always have more than one meaning you know."

He continued, "But of course you know who He is. You know exactly who Jehovah is. Don't bother lying to me! You heard Noah preach, not to mention Lamech, Enoch and Methuselah. You not only chose to ignore their warnings, but you identified the Most High as the enemy of your goddess. Don't use ignorance as an excuse to me! I invented that excuse. Your separation from God and those who are forever at peace is your own choosing. And that separation is forever. I am your Master, now and for eternity. No, don't try that 'I didn't know any better' line."

More laughter. "And don't worry about your favorite child. You taught Zalith well. She will choose the same path and will join you eventually. But then, I probably won't let you see her. We wouldn't want any happy reunions."

"My Lord, is this it? Is this the reward I have for faithful service? Where is my goddess, my beloved one?"

He promptly transformed into a vision of Inanna, with flowing robes and hair. His sarcastic laughter became the familiar benevolent voice of her revelations.

"I can tell you another secret you'll never be able to reveal to anyone. I, or actually we, lose in the end."

Not wanting to pursue that insight, Dehlia still continued her questions, "And where is Mother Eve? The one that you transformed into our goddess in the Garden."

"Why should I tell you?"

"Why do you tell me anything?"

"Because you entertain me. Remember I lie, its what I do best."

Lucifer motioned with his hand and the rock wall transformed into a vision of a man and woman. They appeared to be completely blissful. She saw colors beyond her experience; so intense she could feel them. Joyful music filled the air. Dehlia was consumed with jealousy.

"My Lord, how can I go there?"

"You can't. There is a great distance between where you are and where they are that you cannot cross. You made your choice. There is no repentance in the afterlife", he said with a smirk.

"But who are they?"

"Adam and Eve."

"But she appears to be only human."

"Of course. She is."

"You're lying."

"Maybe. Look despicable one; there is only One God, The Most High. No mere human can become a god. Even angels cannot become gods. I know; I tried. Yes, I am powerful, I have legions of demons under my command, and I have been given a time of dominion, but I am not like the Most High."

"But all my life, I was told if I followed the faith, made the sacrifices, fulfilled the sacraments, I also would become a goddess." Dehlia complained.

"I don't know where such ideas came from. Oh, wait a minute. Yes I do. From me! Like I said, I know I lose eventually, but my destruction is sometime in the future. I also am aware of the prophecy of a Redeemer and my defeat. In the meantime, I amuse myself by deceiving hordes of lowly humans into following me. Even those who have chosen the Most High are not immune to my influence. I love to destroy their self-confidence, bring discord to their relationships, to see their ambitions stifled and their missions failed. And what about those who reject the Most High? Their eternal torture gives me such great joy. Their worship and adulation while on earth is flattering, but you can see where it gets them."

***

Dehlia turned and immediately she was in her Aunt Millicent's parlor. Both she and Aunt Millie were dressed in formal white and lavender-trimmed afternoon tea dresses. Dehlia had a lavender ribbon tied around her waist, with a big bow in the back.

"I haven't dressed like this since I was twelve."

The scene was pleasant, the room neat and sunny

"Sit down Dearie and have some tea." Aunt Millie poured the steaming tea into two of the delicate china cups Dehlia remembered so well from her childhood. The cups were just as beautiful now with their perfectly painted violet flowers, climbing green vines and gold-trimmed rims. She suddenly recalled stealing one and hiding it in her bedroom with her dolls. *Why am I feeling guilty now, I never felt guilty before? I needed it! The toy teacups were fine for the dolls, but I needed a real one and Aunt Millie's were so pretty. Besides she had a whole set and only used two or three at a time, anyway.*

Aunt Millie smiled at her again and motioned for her to sit down. "Do have some biscuits, 'Lia. They are fresh from the oven and I have some orange marmalade, just like you always liked. Let's have a little chitchat."

Dehlia's mouth was watering. The biscuits did look delicious and for all she knew she hadn't eaten for centuries. Or was it minutes?

She sat down at the table. The centerpiece, a small bouquet of violets, nodded their flower heads and smiled at her. The smell of fresh biscuits, citrus and butter, mixed with just the perfect amount of flower essence soothed her. *Things are definitely looking up. Maybe Hell isn't all bad. This is just like the countless afternoons Aunt Millie spent teaching me how to interpret tealeaves.*

"But you know, 'Lia, I did wonder just a little when you actually believed Noah about the Flood. I thought I might loose the pleasure of your eternal company. Fortunately, I had made some of my best false prophecies to keep you on the right, or should I say wrong, path – or does that even matter? Strange how tea leaves and chicken guts can influence a person more than one of God's greatest prophets. After all, imperfect imitations and partial truths are my specialty."

"You're not my Aunt Millie, are you?"

"Where's my teacup?"

"What?" Dehlia put down the biscuit dripping with melted butter and sweetly tart marmalade she was just about to enjoy.

"You know what teacup, dear. Did you bring it back?"

"Well of course not. Everything of the old world is destroyed. And I see more cups over in your hutch." Dehlia started to take a bite of the biscuit. She couldn't wait; it looked and smelled so wonderful!

"Then no biscuits for you!" The biscuit flew out of her hand and hit the wall.

The walls started spinning, slowly at first than faster and faster. All of the biscuits, condiments, center piece and tea set hit the wall and blended into a swirling blur. She looked at Millie. The flesh was beginning to melt from her elongated and ghoul-like face. Millie was talking, but slowly and in a deep voice, "did you think you could steal teacups with no.." Then Millie's dissolving body flew into the rapidly rotating wall as well. Splat! Her voice continued as she blended into the revolving goo, "…con..se..quences?"

All of the lovely lavender and violet colors were fading into a horribly ugly watered down black-green. It was if the colors were trying to be vibrant but someone had painted a blackwash over them. *What is that smell? It's horrible.* She covered her face with her now ugly tea dress, but the odor was penetrating everything. *Its like someone left a million cut violets in the vase about a week too long and mixed it with rotten fish liver.*

"I can't stand it"

Then the noise started. She put the dress down from her face to see what the sound might be. It reminded her of the raindrops she heard hitting her roof when the Flood started. Then she realized what it was she was hearing. The walls had stopped spinning and the conglomerated liquid that had been held to the walls by the rotating motion was now dripping onto the floor. Each drip was larger and louder than the previous one. The once square room was now a shrinking circle. The drips were coalescing as she realized the oozing liquid was also the source of the stench; she became surrounded by ugly stinking puddles of violet-black slime.

Then the slime puddles began to take shape. Five forms rose up. They were becoming recognizable. She gasped – *No, impossible.* They were giant violets: indescribably ugly, but still violets. They had leaf-shaped arms and legs. The flower petals covered their heads. *No the petals are their heads. Whatever, they have teeth, and large sharp ones.*

The one closest to her opened its mouth and flames streamed out. She collapsed in fear. She crouched in a fetal position, her arms covering her head. She couldn't bear to look at them.

One spoke to the others, " wouldn't it have made more sense for us to be snapdragons, not violets?"

They all laughed, "Or maybe nasty-urchims."

"You're right; violets are such 'pansy' flowers"

"Good one. What should we do first? Rip her apart or burn her? He didn't give us very specific instructions."

"Doesn't matter, she can't die again. That's the good part. We can torture her all we want, she will be able to suffer eternally, and no death can relieve her pain."

Chapter 18

The Ark, 2348, BC

Naamah found Debra in the goat pen and her heart went out to her. She sat down beside her and just let Debra decide when she was ready to talk. "Mother Naamah, I can't stay with Shem, he…he…doesn't really love me."

"Of course he does, dear. You have just had a little quarrel. Every couple has them once in awhile."

"You and Noah don't."

"Yes, we do. Of course we do. We've just gotten to know each other over the past one hundred years. We have learned not to irritate one another, that's all." Naamah secretly wished that she could arouse any type of emotional passion from Noah. If pressed, she would have to describe their marriage as 'friendly' or more like a 'business partnership'. But she didn't want to burden Debra with her problems; besides she wasn't sure that she wanted to admit she had any problems, not even to Noah.

"Naamah, last night when Shem was holding me, he called me by another woman's name."

Naamah could certainly relate to that. She had been called Zara so many times that she hardly noticed anymore. She sighed. "Debra, that hurts, but it is hardly grounds for ending a marriage, especially to such a man as Shem."

"But Naamah, he didn't even know he did it. It was so natural to him, like he told this woman he loved her all the time."

"Well, dear, that just proves my theory."

"What theory?"

"That when men are thinking about love-making, their brains are not connected to their mouths." Naamah was heartened to see a little smile from Debra.

"I'll do the milking and you finish cleaning and feeding. Then we'll get cleaned up and you can help me in the kitchen. I want to tell you something." Naamah decided it was time to tell Debra about Zara.

***

Soon Debra was busy scrubbing and peeling potatoes and carrots. Naamah had made her curious and she was getting just a little impatient. *She probably just wants to lecture me about the sanctity of marriage, but then, it was almost like she wanted to confide in me.* "What did you want to tell me, Mother Naamah?" she finally asked.

"I am having difficulty finding just the right words. I want to tell you something about Noah and me, but I don't want you to think that I am in anyway unhappy or jealous."

Jealous! What was she talking about? Surely godly Noah has done nothing to make her jealous. Now she was even more curious. She looked at her mother-in-law quizzically, waiting for her to explain.

"Noah was married before he and I were married. She divorced him when he started to build the Ark and she soon married Noah's friend, a carpenter who had been helping him with the ship's construction. Noah still loves her and he calls me by her name all the time, even now. At first, it really bothered me; and I have to admit it still bothers me. But Debra, it doesn't mean that we don't have a good life together. And I know that he loves me, but in a different way. I can't explain it well, but sometimes I think it is better to really love someone, even if that love is not wholly returned, than to be loved. Of course mutual love is best, I guess. But you can never truly experience love if it only stays on an emotional and physical level. I think what I am trying to say is that true love, a love beyond the realm of romantic love, doesn't depend upon being returned. That doesn't mean feelings aren't involved in a relationship and that you can't be hurt, but you need to put things into their proper perspective."

"Naamah, I had no idea. You seem so happy and cheerful all the time."

"I am happy. Noah and I are very happy."

Debra was confused. How could she say that? How could she be happy with a man who didn't love her the way she loved him? She silently busied herself preparing the vegetables and tried to understand a love that didn't need to be returned.

***

Naamah was also a little confused and worked silently. Who was this woman that Shem was so preoccupied with that he unconsciously called his wife by her name? As far as she knew, Debra was Shem's first and only relationship. Maybe Shem had a secret city life like Ham and had some lingering memories.

She broke the silence. "Debra, don't jeopardize your marriage by being jealous over a woman who no longer exists and was probably just a passing fling, only a mostly forgotten memory. I know that Shem loves you. Besides, you're alive and she, along with the rest of the world is dead."

Debra's expression hardened. "I *wish* she were dead." She wiped her hands, dropped her towel on the counter and left the kitchen.

Naamah stared at the soup she was making in disbelief as she contemplated this new information. So, Shem was apparently infatuated with one of her other daughters-in-law. This couldn't be good, things were getting strained enough. They were all getting on each other's nerves and tempers were flaring over trivial differences. But this wasn't trivial. She could only hope this infatuation was only that. She couldn't imagine Shem actually having an affair, especially with one of his brother's wives. Then she remembered seeing Zalith sitting close to Shem with her hand on his thigh, talking secretly with him. She had thought it a little inappropriate, and also that Shem looked a little uncomfortable, but really didn't think that much about it, until now. She couldn't help saying a desperate prayer, "Please God, get us off this boat before something awful happens."

Chapter 19
The Ark, 2348 BC

After Noah lifted the ban on sex, Japheth hurriedly led Cassie to their room. He was anxious and excited, so much so that he didn't notice Cassie's reluctance. When they finally reached their destination, down the long corridor of the living quarters, Japheth closed the door and enveloped Cassie in a passionate embrace. When he began to kiss her, she turned her head and pulled away.

"Jay, please wait. I'm not sure that I want to do this."

"What are you saying? We have been waiting months for this."

"Well… maybe you have. I.. I.." she stammered.

"Don't you still love me?"

"Oh Jay, of course I do. You are my whole life. Literally. I'm not sure that I 'm ready to share you with anybody, even our own children. And motherhood is so….." Her voice trailed off as she was searching for the right words while the whole time Japheth was trying to kiss her shoulders and loosen her clothing.

"Stop that! I'm trying to talk to you!"

"Are you trying to say that you don't want children?"

"No. Yes. Not now. This is just so sudden. I was perfectly happy the way things were". Sharing his bed and his embraces without the responsibility of actually fulfilling the sexual aspect of their marriage was a relief to her.

"Just knowing that you love me for me and not just someone to have sex with has meant everything to me."

"Cassie, you know that I love you. I don't understand." Cassie could see the hurt and frustration in his eyes.

"Japheth, look at me. If we were back in Tymorrah, I would still be considered a child myself. I just turned eighteen a few months before we were married. Nobody that I knew got married and had children at eighteen! None of my sisters did. They were still having fun and enjoying their youth. Did you think about marriage when you were eighteen? Were you ready to be a father then?"

"Well I guess that's true. At eighteen, I was still in school and every spare moment was spent working on the Ark. But aren't girls different? Don't all girls want to be mothers as soon as possible? And don't you feel honored that God chose you to repopulate the world?" Japheth suddenly stopped himself from saying more. Even to his ears, everything he said came out wrong. He didn't know if he felt more shocked, confused, hurt, rejected or angry.

They had never had a serious disagreement before, and to him, this was very serious. Not only did he want children, but also he wanted to be a husband to Cassie. Apparently she only wanted him to be a friend, maybe even just a father replacement.

"Cassie, I love you. I can wait. Goodnight. I am going to sleep."

***

Cassie felt the tone of anger in his voice; it didn't match his words. She sat down on the edge of the bed and slowly got under the blankets, not even changing into her nightclothes. She suddenly felt awkward about changing in front of him and was relieved when Japheth turned down the lamp after he rather quickly got ready to go to sleep. She was waiting for him to embrace her, to fall asleep in his arms as she usually did, but Jay stayed as far away from her as possible, on his side of the bed with his back turned to her.

Tears welled up in Cassie's eyes; she felt alone, rejected. She had no one to talk to about her personal problems; she desperately missed her mother and sisters. She sighed as tears streamed down her face. She decided to ask Jay's mother for some advice. *But should she? She's his mother and would most likely side with him; after all she's constantly saying how much she wants grandchildren. Oh well, what have I got to lose? Jay hates me now; things can't get any worse. Don't my feelings mean anything to him?*

Cassie didn't sleep very well, partly because she was trying to sort out her feelings, but mostly because she wanted to make sure that she was up and gone before Japheth woke up. She looked for Naamah, but couldn't find her in the kitchen. She busied herself with her animal duties, but her mind was on her husband. *Why did I act like that last night?* She didn't really know, but she knew she didn't want to be physically intimate with Japheth for some reason. *But why? The thought of pregnancy isn't even the main reason, but I am not sure exactly what that main reason is. The pregnancy issue was just the first thing that popped into my head after Noah mentioned it at dinner and my youth seemed to make it a plausible argument. We've had sex before and I got through it.* She smiled to herself. *Japheth probably wouldn't like the phrase, 'got through it'.* She felt a little claustrophobic at times during lovemaking, and mostly just wanted it to end quickly. She never mentioned this to him, and he, lost in his passion, never noticed.

Cassie was secretly elated when Noah told them to refrain from procreation. Like she told Jay last night, she liked things the way they were. In fact, she loved everything about living on this floating zoo. She enjoyed the company of the animals and she enjoyed taking care of them. The routine was trying, but knowing what to do and when to do it was comforting. She had to admit she also enjoyed Naamah taking care of her. *Maybe that's the reason for my reluctance: I'm just afraid to take on the responsibility of running my own household, to be the wife and mother. What if I fail? I don't even know how to cook! And if I did, how does one decide what to cook? I need to talk to Jay. I hope I can make him understand.*

During breakfast and lunch Cassie quietly sat beside her husband. He didn't try to hold her hand under the table, as he sometimes liked to do. He didn't even look at her eyes. She knew he was hurting, but she didn't know what to do. She was afraid if she made advances to him, she would be rejected. He wasn't behaving like he even liked her, let alone loved her. *He's the man; he's the older, more experienced one. He needs to be the one to apologize and make things right again. I don't know how to deal with this! He's being selfish and unreasonable. Certainly this isn't my fault.*

***

After lunch Cassie volunteered to help Naamah with the laundry. Naamah was a little suspicious that something was wrong, since Cassie had never seemed the least bit interested in domestic duties in the past. She would always helpfully comply if asked to help, but never just dove into a task the way Debra did. Naamah noticed at the table Cassie and Japheth weren't acting like themselves, not even looking at each other. She was a little surprised at their coolness. She would have expected them to be cooing like turtledoves today. *Did they have a fight too? O Lord, what next?*

Cassie looked at the pile of dirty laundry and then helplessly at Naamah.

"Honey, surely you know how to wash clothes. Didn't your mother teach you?"

Tears started to run down Cassie's face. "We had servants and my sisters…"

"Now, now, dear, its only laundry. It will just take a few moments to learn. Water, soap, scrub, rinse and hang; that's about it."

93

"Its not the laundry, I mean, I do want to help you and I do want to learn, but just now I need to talk. Last night, I couldn't, well I couldn't…" She took a deep breath.

"This isn't easy for me to talk about. I just didn't want Jay to make love to me. I don't know what's wrong. I told him that I wasn't ready to be a mother, and I think that's true, but something else is …" Cassie's lip was quivering and she couldn't finish her sentence. Holding back her tears, she bit her lip and took in a sharp breath through clenched teeth.

Naamah didn't hear the muffled ending of Cassie's words. She assumed that fear of pregnancy was Cassie's main concern. That was a relief, after her conversation with Debra this morning she was half afraid that Cassie was going to tell her she was in love with Shem. "Cassie, don't worry, I can help you with not getting pregnant. You probably know that I was older than most women when they marry. I wanted to make sure that I had children right away; so I talked to many women, especially my sisters-in-law and the midwives for my nieces. They explained to me that there are times when women are more likely to get pregnant, just like there are times when the farm animals are more likely to conceive. You just need to follow that timing in reverse, avoid love making during those more fertile times. I'll help you make out a schedule. I will be right back; I'm going to put these clothes away."

"Mother Naamah. Please don't go, there's more," Cassie desperately cried out to Naamah as she started to leave. Cassie started weeping again but managed to blurt out,

"I don't, I just don't feel pretty enough for him. I am turning into a hideous ugly monster, and I don't want him to see me with my clothes off…"

"Cassie, what are you talking about? I see his face light up when you come into the room. He adores you."

"He adores the old Cassie" She grabbed one of the dirty shirts and wiped her face and blew her nose. "When Japheth first met and fell in love with me, I was tiny. And now look at me! He called me his little wood nymph. I keep growing. My feet are like rudders and I'm too tall for all my clothes. I'm almost as tall as he is. I bump my knees when I try to sit at the table. Everything is growing except where I want things to grow. My legs are too skinny and my chest is too flat. My hair doesn't do what I want it to. It's always in my face, which I guess is good, because it covers my freckles and my big ugly nose. When I look at

94

Zalith and Debra I feel so ugly, so awkward and inferior. They make me feel like a giant."

"Cassie, did you tell Japheth how you are feeling? I am sure he will be able to reassure you that he still thinks that you are attractive."

"No. After I told him that I didn't want to have sex with him, he got mad and is barely speaking to me."

"You really didn't want to? Not even after all these months?" *that's odd.*

"Cassie, how old are you?"

"Almost nineteen."

"Well no wonder you're still growing. You don't even have all your teeth! Honey, don't worry about the sex. All your parts are just not working yet. You and Japheth have years and years to learn how to please each other. Remember, God has ordained marriage for men and women to enjoy each other, to be one flesh, not just to make babies. And Honey, don't worry about being pleasing to Jay. At this point, just being there is enough for him. But Japheth needs to be patient with you, and you, my dear, need to realize that sometimes men get sex and love mixed up. They take it very personally when rejected. Let him know that you are still attracted to him and that you still care for him. You need to smooth his ruffled feathers. Especially Jay, he has always been so sensitive. There is an old saying that the women in my town used to say, 'If you want your man to treat you like a woman, treat him like a man'."

"But that's just it, I don't know how. And I don't feel like a woman, anyway."

Naamah smiled at her, "Let's start with the basics, and this shouldn't be difficult, Cassie, because you really are very pretty. A new feminine outfit and a new hair-do will make you feel that way. And Japheth will be flattered that you are trying to look attractive for him. Maybe you can stop thinking about what you look like and try to relax a little."

"I'm sorry. It's just a little embarrassing and weird talking about my intimate moments to my husband's mother."

Cassie shyly lowered her eyes and then looked up. Her face brightened with a slight smile, "I seemed to have missed on which level the clothing stores and hair salons are located."

Naamah returned her smile. "We'll need to enlist the help of your sisters-in-law. I am sure they have something you could wear and we can alter it if we need to. And Zalith can do wonders with her own hair. I am sure that she will help you with yours. Speaking of Zalith, can you take this pile of clothes to her?"

"Mother Naamah, you have been working this whole time! I can't ….. I am just not ready to run a household, I don't know how."

"Dear, just take it slowly. I'll help, and Jay doesn't expect you to know everything at once."

"I really don't know what Jay expects from me."

"Cassie, do you want me to talk to Jay? Try to explain things to him."

"No!" She said emphatically, stomping her foot. "I don't want his sympathy! I just want him to, to... I am not sure what I want him to do. I just want him to love me enough to understand what I want without someone telling him."

Cassie left the laundry room and Naamah returned to her work. *I was so busy with preparing the Ark and taking care of my enlarging family that I didn't think much about Cassie's youth. Most girls weren't ready for marriage and the responsibility of house and family until they were well into their thirties. Even if there were servants, someone had to be in charge.* She re- thought that statement. *Actually most modern women were never ready for the responsibility of marriage. They were too interested in themselves, and it seemed they were never satisfied, always looking to get out of one marriage and into another: like Zara.* Then Naamah had to stop herself from feeling resentful, *after all, if Zara didn't leave Noah, I wouldn't have him. But do I really have him?* "Stop it, quit feeling sorry for yourself and get back to work", she said to the shrinking pile of laundry. *I am as bad as Cassie, unsure of myself with unrealistic ideas of love.* She shook her head as if to get her thoughts back. *What's wrong with me? I have lived in Zara's shadow for over a century and seemed to be doing just fine. Its no wonder Cassie was feeling overwhelmed: after all, she is only an awkward and confused teenager. I, on the other hand, have no excuse and no time for self-pity.*

Chapter 20

The Ark, 2348 BC

Cassia gently knocked on Zalith's door. "Zalith, are you there? I have some of Ham's clothes to put away."

Zalith quickly covered her book of spells she was studying and opened the door. "Thanks, Cassie."

Cassie handed Zalith the clean shirts and started to leave, but then turned back.

"Zalith, I was wondering if you could do me a favor, help me with something."

Zalith assumed she wanted help with some type of domestic chore or animal related activity, both of which she tried to avoid. "I will help if I can, but you know I am not very strong, and the animals make me sneeze."

"Oh, no, nothing like that. It's a fashion problem, of sorts."

Zalith was intrigued. "Come in, come in. What fashion problem?"

"Well, you know you always look so pretty, and I want to try to look more attractive for my husband."

Zalith smiled. "I have just the thing." She opened a trunk full of neatly folded colorful silks. She pulled out a pair of sheer rose-colored harem pants, with a dark rose halter-top that matched the waistband.

"These should be alluring and revealing enough to get his attention."

"Oh, Zalith. Those are beautiful, but I would be too embarrassed to wear them. Wherever did you get all these gorgeous clothes? The night that you came to Noah's house you didn't have anything with you, did you?"

"Ham bought me most of them, but some are things that he picked up for me from my mother's house." Zalith thought that maybe she should explain that a little more. "I just wanted her to know that I was alright."

Zalith didn't need to bother to keep her story straight; Cassia was too busy admiring the silks. Zalith feared that Cassie might figure out that a family so poor they had to sell their daughter didn't seem to equate with all these expensive clothes, but Cassie didn't seem to notice.

Something on the bottom of the trunk caught Cassie's eye. She hurriedly pulled out a shimmering light blue nightdress. "Zalith, my mother wove this! Or at least one of her workers wove it. I can tell by her trademark decorative selvage," She continued in an excited voice "She invented that type of edging to eliminate the need for a bulky hem. She didn't like the way that dressmakers ruined the flow of her beautiful lightweight fabrics by folding it under to finish it, so she devised a pre-finished edge. My mother was a textile genius, not to mention a famous designer, too. "

"Cassie, I can't believe it. Are you Cassandra's daughter? The most sought after dress designer in the kingdom?"

"Yes. So you know about my mother's work?"

"Of course. But I also heard that she, her workshop and her entire family were destroyed by a Nephilim raid."

Cassie's face clouded over. "I wasn't home when it happened. But let's not talk about that. We were having such a good time."

Zalith was amazed that tomboy Cassie was the daughter of a fashion icon. While Cassie continued to admire Zalith's lingerie wardrobe, Zalith pondered how this new information might someday be of use to her.

"Cassia, can you make silk?"

"If I had the fibers and a loom. But silk isn't that easy. There is something about worms and mulberry leaves. But I think Naamah brought cotton and flax seeds. And of course we have the raw materials for wool, angora and mohair from the animals. I don't know about the dyes. Maybe Naamah brought some. I hadn't thought about new clothes."

Zalith smiled to herself and thought that was obvious. " So you would really be too embarrassed to wear the harem outfit? Even for your husband?" She was a little confused about just what Cassia wanted.

"Yes. Even if I wanted to, it would be too small I'm sure. Do you have anything else? Something looser? Something longer? What about the night dress from my mother's silk?" She held it up against her; the shimmering blue fabric with silver metallic highlights streamed down towards the floor, but stopped about six inches above her ankles.

"Too short… my big ugly feet will stick out."

Zalith laughed. "Chances are Japheth is not going to be looking at your feet. The color is perfect for you. I think you should take it. If you would be more comfortable, be sitting on your bed when he comes into the room. Your intentions will be obvious. Now let's work on your hair and some jewelry. You can wear some of my perfume, too. Before our wedding, Ham wanted to buy me some perfume but he didn't know what I liked, so he just bought several of each at the perfumery. Silly man. But that's good for you, I have plenty to share, and I will most likely never wear the flowery or fruity ones."

Zalith was thoroughly enjoying herself. She braided silver ribbon into Cassia's unruly hair. She then twisted and piled it into a bun on the top of her head and held the bun in place with silver ornaments. Then Zalith pulled some tendrils down to frame her face.

"Cassie, look," Zalith held a mirror up to her.

"How did you do that? I can never do anything with my hair. I don't even look like myself; I look more like one of my older sisters. Do you think Jay will like it?"

"I am sure he'll like it, but to be honest with you, anyone can see that the man is head over heals in love with you. Don't worry so much about it." She went to her drawer and pulled out a brightly colored scarf with a distinctive black and white stripped border.

"Oh, Zalith! I am sure Mother designed that too! Absolutely no one else put together such intense purples, blues, reds and greens with black and white stripes."

Zalith was getting a little annoyed with Cassie's fixation on her mother, after all the woman was dead and couldn't produce anymore fabric. "That's nice, she was very talented." *Whatever.* "Just take the scarf and before dinner tie it over your new hairstyle. Keep the hair a surprise for Japheth until tonight when you wear the blue silk. Here, take these silver earrings," she said as she looked through her jewelry box.

Cassie interrupted, "But my ears aren't pierced."

"Oh. Then just take this silver necklace with the sapphire pendant. And here's some eye shadow, liner and lip color. But wait to use it until later. Do you know how?"

"My sisters tried to show me. I can put it on, I just don't know if I want to."

"Just remember that you are doing it for Japheth. You can keep the make-up, nightgown and the scarf, but I need the necklace back. It was a present from my own mother. Come back tomorrow and tell me about your night. I can't wait."

Cassie started to blush and then both Cassie and Zalith impulsively started giggling, the way that only girls can. Neither one had anticipated that the afternoon would turn out to be so enjoyable. Neither one had much to laugh about lately. Cassie left still giggling and closed the door with a smile and a thank you to Zalith.

Zalith smiled as well, as she retrieved her heavy book from its hiding place. *How interesting and convenient. Cassie needs some advice and companionship, and I need a junior priestess to aid me in my worship rituals. I do miss my priestess sisters; we always had such good times talking and laughing at the temple!*

Chapter 21
The Ark, 2348 BC

Ham and Japheth were busy hauling in driftwood and fish in one of the strong huge nets that Noah brought in anticipation of their use after the storm.

Japheth was usually a talkative companion, but he hadn't said much all afternoon. Ham's curiosity was aroused and he was about to ask what the problem was, when Japheth broke the silence.

"You know a lot about women, right? Maybe you can explain something to me."

Ham smiled and said, "Well, as I told you, I do have a good bit of experience with women and many nights of passion when I used to sneak into the city. If you're talking about the physical aspects of a relationship, I can help. But if you are asking me to explain how or why they do things, I wouldn't say that I know much about women."

"I thought that I knew Cassie, as well as I know myself. Last night she was cold and heartless to me. I thought that she wanted children and as soon as possible. She tells me she doesn't. To tell you the truth, I am mystified. I thought she loved me the way I love her, but now I don't know."

"I know enough about women to know that sometimes they say one thing and mean something else. However, they also expect you to know that and to be able to interpret what they really mean. Let's start from the beginning. What exactly happened?" Ham said as they attached the net to the pulley they used to bring up the heavy load to the top story of the huge ship.

"After we left the table, we went to our room, I kissed her and she rejected me."

"So that was it, you just closed the door and kissed her? Well, Brother, that's probably the problem. You knew from our earlier conversation that Dad was probably going to lift that ban. You had been anticipating and thinking about it all day. She had no idea what Dad was going to say. Women aren't always immediately ready for sex, the way we men are. Go slow, tell her how pretty she is, how much you love her. Other than that, don't say anything."

"By now, doesn't she know that I think she is attractive and that I love her?"

"Never hurts to repeat it. Cassie looks fairly young. I'm guessing she doesn't have much experience in the lovemaking department, and I know that you don't. Do you know that in the city, they had entire brothels where the rich merchants sent their sons just to get ready for marriage?"

"Ham, you never went to such a place, did you?"

"Don't be ridiculous. I never paid for anything!"

They were pulling on the rope in tandem, Japheth working behind Ham so that Ham didn't see the shocked look on Japheth's face. Ham continued after the catch was brought up and the fish put into a holding tank. "The point is there are sexual techniques that need to be learned. But you know, I don't think that is the source of Cassie's reluctance. Besides, I am finding that married love, at least when you love someone as much as I love Zalith, is more than technique. I never knew how different marriage would be from a casual encounter; nor did I realize the level of intimacy that could be attained when two people are totally committed to each other. I also really never thought that I could be faithful to just one person, or that I would even want to. I know we don't have much of a choice in the present circumstances, but if I did, and there were millions of other women still around, I wouldn't trade my relationship with Zalith for any number of nights with them."

"Thanks Ham, I really appreciate your insights." He paused, cleaning the unwanted debris from the net and throwing it overboard. "I guess marriage is forcing all of us to grow up. I sort of expected you to just make fun of me."

"Well, you're usually a good subject for a joke, but neither you or Shem are in the mood today. Jay, don't scare her away from you. Be more in tune with her feelings. Feelings seem to be more important to women than men can imagine. And whatever you do, don't force her. You don't want her to hate you."

***

At dinner, Japheth was relieved to see that Cassie seemed much more relaxed. She even smiled at him. "What's with the scarf?" he asked her, mostly just to make conversation.

"I had to wash my hair. When I was taking care of the parrots, one of them gave me an unexpected present. I didn't want to come to dinner with bird droppings on my head."

"No, I suppose not. But I don't remember it, where did you get it?" Jay asked. He really didn't care where the scarf came from, but he was glad that it gave him something to talk to her about.

102

"Zalith gave it to me."

While they were eating, Cassie reached for his hand under the table and gave him a reassuring squeeze. Japheth was now totally confused. At lunch, she acted like she hated him; now she is acting like nothing happened. *Ham is right, women can't be figured out*, he thought as he broke his bread into his vegetable soup.

"Jay, can you stay here and talk to your brothers before you come to our room? I have a surprise for you", she told him as she got up to leave.

Maybe I am making too much of this. And surely her talking the other day about being married to one of my brothers meant nothing. Didn't it?

Chapter 22

The Ark, 2348 BC

Cassie excitedly changed her clothes, smoothed out her hair and applied the eye make-up and lip color. *Someday I am going to have to tell Jay about the last time I put on make-up, maybe he will be more understanding.* She wished Zalith had given her something to hide her freckles, but then they wouldn't be so prominent in the lamplight.

She looked into her mirror. *I hope that Jay likes this; I really do look different.* Suddenly she gasped and dropped the mirror. *But if he likes it, that means that he didn't really like me before. What am I doing? Poor Jay,* she smiled to herself, *he can't win. If he likes it, I'll be mad at him and if he doesn't, I'll be mad at him.* Cassie got up to take off the make-up, let down her hair and change back into her old nightgown. She sat back down. *I already told him I have a surprise for him, he'll be wondering what it is.*

***

Jay couldn't control his curiosity any longer and went to see what surprise Cassie prepared for him. *Maybe she made a special treat for me as a peace offering, she knows I love sweets, or drew something from the forest.* When he opened the door he immediately forgot Ham's warning about not making any extra comments.

Jay smiled quizzically then jokingly said, "Honey, you look like a harlot."

Cassie covered her face with her hands and turned away from him, her legs drawn up towards her chest. Her shoulders were heaving in what Jay perceived as uncontrolled weeping.

"Cassie, I'm sorry. I didn't mean you don't look nice. I am just not used to seeing you like this, and…. you don't have to dress like this for me. I love you just the way you are."

Still silence from Cassie, and Jay didn't know what to say. "But if you like it, I'll adjust. You can wear all the fancy silks and jewelry that you want." Jay was becoming more and more uncomfortable. He felt that everything he said was just making the situation worse.

"Cassie, please talk to me." He gently turned her towards him and pulled her hands from her face. He was relieved but totally confused to see she was laughing and not crying.

She threw her arms around his neck. "Oh, Jay. I knew that you would say that! It's so ironic, don't you think?"

Jay really didn't see the irony, but decided that "Yes" was a good answer.

"Cassie, you know I didn't have to marry you. Rich young men were becoming scarce in Tymorrah, and I could have had my choice of women. I chose you."

"I know, back then when I was cute and small, but don't you think that I am getting ugly and too tall? How can you love somebody that trips over her own feet all the time?"

"I think that you are the most gorgeous woman I have ever met. And now you are like a beautiful yearling gazelle that hasn't grown into her legs yet. To me, you are becoming more beautiful every day."

"Jay, look at the bottom edge of this dress that Zalith gave me. It's from my mother's shop! Isn't that wonderful?"

Again Jay was totally confused at the rapid change in the conversation, but he again decided that "Yes" was the correct answer.

He pulled her close, but this time he remembered Ham's warning and tried to refrain from overwhelming her with his advances. He kissed the top of her head.

"I like the perfume. What is it? Something citrusy, Hmmm ...Smells good, like fresh cut lemons," he said as he started to kiss her face. "Wait. I'll be right back."

Japheth went to the washbasin and got a wet cloth and a towel. He gently washed her eyes and then kissed them as he removed the eye shadow. When he washed off the lipstick, he couldn't help but kiss her. This time, she kissed him back.

"Jay, please turn off the lamp."

"But..." once again, he decided that "yes" might be the best answer.

Chapter 23
The Ark, 2348 BC

The days gradually turned into weeks as Debra tried to lose herself in her work. She was feeling more and more isolated as she noticed the growing friendship between Cassia and Zalith. Shem had stopped asking her to return to him; in fact he seemed to want to avoid her altogether. They ate their meals silently. Debra was thankful that she and Shem customarily sat across from each other, so that she could avoid him touching her, but it was difficult to avoid his glances. She was careful to return them with her own accusing ones. Naamah was her only confidant, but Debra could tell even she was feeling uncomfortable around her.

After lunch, she heard laughter from one of the rooms near the laundry. When she peeked in, she saw Cassie instructing Naamah and Zalith how to weave contrasting wools into plaids. Debra was hurt and thought it strange and even a little rude of them not to invite her to the lesson.

"Can you girls imagine Noah wearing something so colorful?" Naamah laughingly asked.

Cassie replied, "It will make a nice bedcover. Nice and warm, too. The nights seem to be getting much colder."

"Let's make one for Debra. She needs something to keep her warm these days," Zalith said in an overly sweet sarcastic voice.

"You witch!" Debra exclaimed as she ran away, ignoring Naamah's plea for her to return and join them.

She raced down the corridor, tears streaming down her face. Carelessly she threw herself on her makeshift bed. After a little while she tried to compose herself enough to get back to work and once again went to find comfort with her favorite ewes.

"I really should warn Cassia and Naamah that Zalith is not as innocent as she appears. Maybe she is not even content with two men," she confided to the sheep.

"Yes, you're right. They won't believe me. They would just think that I was drunk and jealous again, like Shem did."

Debra picked up one of the newborn lambs and tried to cuddle him. He was so soft and warm. She wished that she could be as innocent and unaware of the evil in the world as he was. The lamb impatiently wrestled himself away from her to return to his mother.

"You, too?" She despondedly sighed. "I should just swallow my pride and go back to Shem. He's really a good man. Whatever is going on between him and Zalith is surely her doing, not his. I miss him. I miss his warm, strong embrace. I miss the smell of his body. I even miss the smell of the spicy cologne that he wears when he doesn't feel like bathing. I don't want to be alone any longer."

"What do you think, Blackie?" she asked the nearest ewe, who was looking at her intently, waiting for more hay.

"Then it's settled. I'll go back to Shem. Thanks for your help, girls. I didn't really say that did I? I guess I am crazy." She smiled to herself, looking forward to the renewal of her relationship with her husband. She moved on to the next pen, the goats.

Debra looked up to see Naamah with a puzzled expression on her face.

"Hi, Honey. I am glad to see you smiling, but why did you run away from the girls and I? We would have gladly let you help with the weaving. And Zalith felt badly that she might have hurt you, she didn't mean anything by it. She didn't know you were listening"

Even though she highly suspected that Zalith must have seen her and that quip was meant to hurt, Debra decided not to respond negatively; it would just make her depressed again. "Its alright, Mother Naamah. I was just feeling lonely and you all looked so happy without me." Debra didn't want to say any more. She wanted to tell her that she had decided to go back to Shem, but if it didn't work out, Naamah would know that Shem didn't want her.

Naamah went to get more fodder for the goats. When she returned, Debra slowly asked her. "There is something that I am very confused about and maybe you can help me find the answer. Why did God save us, or allow Noah to save us? We don't seem to be any better than those he destroyed."

"God does what He does, and we often don't know why. Don't be so hard on yourself, Debra. God didn't create us to be mindless servants. He gave us the ability to choose Him. And He knows the future, so He knows how we will chose before we do. But even when we do make the correct eternal decision, we still make mistakes in our daily lives. None of us are perfect, not even Shem."

Debra laughed, "That's for sure." She stopped short of saying anything else; after all, Naamah was his mother, but she did change her mind about confiding in Naamah about her plans.

"I was just thinking that I should forgive him, and go back to him. Do you think that he will have me?"

"Of course, Dear. But I wouldn't expect him to be too apologetic. Shem's worst characteristic is his pride. Don't let it stand in the way of your happiness. And remember, God put you on this Ark for a reason, and that reason is probably more important than cleaning goat and sheep pens. Let me know if you need help. I can take over some of your chores, and then you can have more time to spend with Shem."

"Thank you. That's very considerate." Debra was touched but surprised that she would volunteer to take on more work. *Was Naamah also trying to avoid facing her personal problems by staying busy?*

"But you already work twice as hard as anyone else on this ship."

Chapter 24

The Ark, 2348 BC

Zalith got up from her knees, put her goddess away and removed her sacred robes. She was extremely pleased at the progress of her plans to keep Debra and Shem apart. She also was pleased at her progress in gaining Cassie's confidence. After all, she would need Cassie and her future children, especially her daughters, to assist in the new Temple.

But what about Shem? He seems less interested in me. At least he doesn't hold those stupid scripture studies anymore. It was pretty tedious trying to look so interested. I hope his faith in Jehovah is slipping; but in any case at least it seems that his faith in himself is slipping, just like I wanted. But if I am going to win Shem over, I need to get Debra totally out of the picture. At dinner last night, she appeared to be softening; maybe she is considering going back to him. That won't do! And why can't I have two husbands? Ham is fun and he adores me, but Shem seems to be the one to take charge and get things done.

"I am getting tired of hiding everything and being so secretive!" she blurted out in a frustrated voice, as she struggled to hide her hat and robe in the back of her wardrobe.

"Where did I put those potions? Ah, here they are." She rifled through the cloth bags and picked one out.

"This one will knock Debra out long enough to get her overboard."

I should stop talking out loud! Those long cotton skirts should make sure that she sinks. But first I think I need to make her appear just a little more crazy, so that suicide will be the assumed answer for her disappearance. That won't be too difficult, she's so sensitive and emotional. Maybe I can arrange her to "catch" me with Shem. That should do it.

Debra really is weak and stupid; she doesn't deserve to have children. Imagine, a third of the new world descended from her. Who needs a bunch of complaining teary-eyed servants?

Chapter 25
The Ark, 2348 BC

Debra tried to work up enough courage to talk to Shem. *Why am I so afraid of him? I am being silly.* She took a deep breath and forced herself to find him. She expected to find him in the larger animal pens where Shem and his brothers customarily spent the afternoons. She walked up to where he and Ham were cleaning out the Rhino pen. She was too intimated by the huge beasts to enter the pen, so she stayed outside.

"Shem can I talk to you?" She tried to make her request as calmly and gently as she could, to give him a hint of her change of heart.

Shem turned to see her shyly smiling at him, " Sure, Debra" He walked over to where she stood by the sturdy rail.

"But not here, somewhere more private. Our ...I mean your bedroom, before dinner. Is that okay?"

He smiled his engaging smile just as she hoped and imagined he would. She ran off to get ready for their meeting.

Shem returned to his work, grinning from ear to ear.

"Shem, you know that I joke a lot, but I will truly be glad if you and Debra make up. I'll finish the work here; you should go and get cleaned up before she arrives. You reek of sweat and manure."

***

Zalith also searched for Shem in the large animal quarters. She walked gingerly, holding her dress close to her body, so that it didn't get soiled. *I bet I look pretty provocative like this.* She hiked her dress just a little bit higher. She was disappointed to find only Ham. *I probably shouldn't ask him where Shem is, maybe he'll tell me.*

"Hi, Darling. I thought that I would just see what it is that you do down here." she replied to his look of surprise. He walked over to meet her.

"Can't keep away from me, huh? You look incredible." Ham said as he began to embrace her.

"Don't touch me! You are all dirty and smelly."

"That's why I am working by myself. Shem went to get cleaned up because Debra was just here and asked to talk to him before dinner in their room. I hope that means they will patch things up and everyone won't be so tense, and we can all get back to normal."

"Ham! That is good news. Bye."

"Zalith wait! Two minutes, that's all I get? Stay here with me; we're all alone. It's a good thing we're all alone, because when you hold your dress like that anyone can see the entire outline of your thigh, including that dagger you always wear. C'mon stay and let's make love on the hay pile."

"I don't think so. Bye, I don't like it here. Too, well you know, just too…icky"

What luck! What perfect timing! Inanna must be arranging this meeting between the three of us, Zalith thought to herself as she hurriedly changed into a light pink silk dress. It wasn't as revealing as some of her outfits, but it was so thin and clingy that it didn't leave much to the imagination. *Shem will think that I look ravishing and Debra will be insanely jealous. Fortunately, I know that Ham and the others are busy elsewhere. Everything is working out so well! Even if Debra is already there, it will still look very suspicious for me to show up at his room, dressed like this. I'll be shocked that she is there. It will appear as if Shem and I meet like this all the time. What fun!*

Zalith confidently knocked on Shem's door.

***

"Come in, Debra" Shem said, trying to sound as normal as possible.

Zalith opened the door, stepped in and then closed it again.

"Zalith? What are you doing here?" Shem was shocked that she would come to his room, alone and dressed as she was. *Does she know how seductive she looks? Is she trying to seduce me?*

"Zalith, you have to leave. Immediately! I'm expecting Debra."

"Shem, I need to talk to you about something."

Shem interrupted, "You can talk to me later; and bring Ham with you."

"Don't you want to be alone with me? Are you afraid that something might happen?" she coyly asked him.

Shem ignored her question, walked past her and opened the door. "Now please go!"

Zalith walked towards the door as Shem held it open, but instead of walking through it she threw her arms around his neck and said, "Shem, I know that you are attracted to me, as I am to you. I am open to bringing our friendship to a physical level. A level of true intimacy."

Shem took her hands from his neck and pushed her away from him. He kept her at a safe distance by continuing to hold her hands in his, but

114

at elbow length. "Zalith, I really don't have time for this. You are only attracted to me because I am so very different from Ham. I think that you are seeking the spiritual enlightenment in me that is missing in Ham. We both need to help him grow."

Zalith was trying to get close to him again and Shem was losing his patience with her, becoming angry.

"I am not going to compromise my marriage. I don't want to hurt Debra and I don't want to hurt my brother. Do you even know what you are saying? A physical relationship between us is not going to happen. When you get over this silly infatuation, you will thank me."

Zalith laughed, "Silly infatuation! I can show you things that Debra couldn't even imagine. She turned slightly, making sure he could view the outline of her body beneath her clinging silk.

"It might even help your marriage, broaden your horizons." She broke free of his grip, and kissed him passionately on the lips.

When they heard Debra's shocked scream, they both turned to see her in the doorway.

"Shem, we really shouldn't do this anymore." Zalith said in an accusingly audible whisper. She broke away from Shem and rushed past Debra.

"Debra, I am sorry. It just happened," she tearfully apologized as she broke away from Shem on her way out.

Debra stood in the doorway for a few seconds before she ran away.

Shem sat in shocked silence on the edge of his bed. Just when he thought everything might return to normal, his life turned upside down again. So many questions were racing in his mind. *What must Debra think of me? Did I lead Zalith on? Did I make her think that I wanted her? I did want her, but not really. It was just a fantasy. Wasn't it? Besides, I haven't even thought about Zalith since Debra left me.* He stood up. *I should run after Debra. Explain to her, or at least try to make her understand what's going on. He sat back down. She won't believe me. At least one question was answered today: Zalith is not as innocent as she appears. Maybe I should tell Debra she was right about that. Well, maybe not. I don't think she has any doubts about Zalith's lack of innocence.*

I suspect that Zalith planned that whole scene, but why? Why should she want to make trouble between Debra and I? Surely she doesn't think that there is any future for her and I. Maybe the townspeople she grew up around changed partners frequently, but she must know that Noah's family isn't like that. I do want to go to Debra, hold her, and tell her that I love her. But I can't. She hates me now. She would only make sarcastic accusations. Reluctantly, Shem got up and went to dinner. *I wonder what Debra was going to say to me, anyway. How dare Debra just jump to conclusions! Didn't she hear me tell Zalith to leave?*

Chapter 26

The Ark, 2348 BC

Shem sat at his place at the dinner table and anxiously awaited Debra's appearance. She never came. Everyone was looking at him for an explanation for her absence. "I guess Debra isn't feeling well and is going to skip dinner tonight." Zalith smiled triumphantly at him. Every one else just accepted that explanation and began to eat after Noah said the customary blessing.

Noah smiled contentedly and said "Well maybe we'll have a little one here soon."

Everyone, especially Naamah, looked at Noah in wonderment. She ruefully smiled and asked herself, *is he really that oblivious? No wonder he hasn't asked me about Shem and Debra's problems. He hasn't even noticed. But then, he is busy. So busy! Oh, my! What if Debra is pregnant and the baby isn't Shem's. Good heavens! what am I saying? These are Noah's sons, not my promiscuous nephews and nieces*

Naamah excused herself to check on Debra and take her some food. She found her in her storage room.

"Debra, what's wrong? You were so happy this afternoon."

"Naamah, I told him that I wanted to talk to him, that I would meet him in his room before dinner and when I arrived *they* were kissing. He knew that I was coming."

"Debra, I know Shem. Even if by some stretch of the imagination, he were having a fling, he wouldn't throw it in your face like that. He might be stubborn and at times, self-righteous, but he is not cruel. There must be some other explanation. Really."

"Then why didn't he come after me and try to explain himself? I waited. I so desperately wanted him to."

"Debra, I don't know. But you can't just hide in here. This boat is too small to avoid him for long. And we won't be here forever. Do you want to shut us all out and be alone for the rest of your life?"

Debra turned away from her, "Yes. Please go."

Chapter 27
The Ark, 2348 BC

Cassia was looking for her favorite green tunic when she came across the make-up that Zalith gave her. She turned to Japheth who was sitting on the bed, putting on his shoes. "Jay, I feel that I need to tell you something that happened to me a while ago."

"What? More drug experiences?"

"No, actually I didn't take the drugs and I didn't drink the wine that night, even though my sisters said it would make it easier."

"OK, you have my attention. Make what easier?"

"Sex, I guess."

"Cassie! I thought that I was the first. Did you lie to me?" Jay said in a hurt and almost angry tone.

"You were. Just let me start at the beginning. My older brothers and sisters, you know that I was the youngest, were always going to parties and they seemed to have such a good time and enjoy themselves so much that I wanted to go with them. My sisters would come home hung-over and exhausted, but by the next day, they were so talkative and excited about this boy and that boy and whom they might marry and who was the best looking and maybe that I was old enough to come with them the next time. My parents finally gave the OK and we spent the whole day dressing and doing our hair and make-up. It made me feel so mature. My sisters told me just to try and relax and enjoy myself. They had an escort for me, a friend of our brothers who thought I was cute. They wanted me to smoke some marijuana and drink some wine so that I would be more in a 'party mood'. Anyway, I didn't because I didn't want anything to dull my senses.

When we got to the house where the party was, everything and everybody was so festive. My date was so nice to me; he kept saying that he 'wanted to be with me'. I didn't know what he was talking about exactly, so when he suggested that we go somewhere to be alone, I just went with him to one of the side rooms. Of course, now I know what he meant. But, anyway, when he started kissing me and tearing my clothes off, I panicked. I screamed and told him to stop. He threw me on the bed and told me to be quiet, that it was embarrassing. Just then my brother, Thomas, rushed in, pulled him off of me and punched him in the face.

'C'mon Cassie, I'm taking you home', Thomas said.

119

My date pulled himself up to his knees. He was genuinely surprised at Tom's actions, and said, 'Tom you should have warned me, I didn't know you had a thing for her. I see you like to keep things in the family.' Tom punched him again, this time he stayed down.

"Cassie, that creep is lucky that he is already dead. I would kill him."

"Jay, it's OK. Nothing really happened. It just scared me, but I'm over it. Mostly. I really wanted to talk to you about my brother, and what he said to me on the way home. We had a long talk, actually about your father."

"My father? Cassie, as usual you are confusing me. I am still trying to absorb the fact that you went to an orgy. What about my father?"

"I'm getting to that. I was upset that I was acting like such a baby, and I did feel so out of place at the party. My sisters said those parties were the best way to find a husband; and now I thought that all the men would avoid me and I would live alone the rest of my life. Thomas reassured me that it was nothing to worry about, that our parents were wealthy enough that I didn't have to worry about finding a husband; a husband would find me."

"My brother," Tears welled up in her eyes and her lip started to quiver.

Jay went to her, gently took her hand and led her over to sit beside him on the edge of their bed.

"It's OK. You don't have to talk about it anymore," Jay said, still holding her hand.

"...its not that I don't want to talk about it, Jay, I just miss my family. They were good people and I wish I had let you meet them. Maybe you could have become friends with my father and convinced him to give up the pharmaceutical businesses. Maybe they could be on the Ark with us now."

"Don't think like that. It would've most likely been just as you said. They would've been polite to me and then teased you when I left. But Cassie, the danger of opposing the Nephilim wasn't a secret, nor was the destruction of the earth. My Father preached to the town for years."

"Yes, but you are different. Maybe they would have listened to you. OK. I'm Ok. Let me get back to my story."

Jay let go of her hand, but still sat beside her. Cassie dried her tears and continued.

"My brother was silent for a while; he seemed to be deep in thought and concentrating on driving the horses. Finally, he spoke. He told me that he was beginning to feel that our parents were wrong: that there was more to life than enjoying yourself and making money. He said that every chance he got, he went into town to listen to your father preach. I was surprised; he seemed to be just as interested in having a good time as he always was. I hadn't noticed a change in him. He declared that one of these days he was going to stop the party life and join Noah. Well, that day never came. He was murdered along with the rest of my family."

Cassie turned towards Jay and looked intently into his eyes. "Do you think that my brother is in paradise? Is there even such a place? Is there really a hell? Or maybe *there* is just eternal nothingness, as my parents believed."

"Whoa! Too many questions that I can't answer. Cassie, I've found that just accepting what my father says is best. He knows. God talks to him."

"But my father always laughed at Noah, and other people say that their gods talk to them, too."

"Cassie, look at the reality of the situation. Wouldn't you say that my father was right and yours wrong? And those other people who said they talk to their gods, they're all dead."

"Maybe, we don't know of any reality outside of this boat. I don't want to believe that my entire family is in a horrible place called Hell. They were good people, they never harmed anyone."

"Alright. Let's talk to Dad and Shem. But keep the questions hypothetical. I don't want them to know just how reprobate your family was or that you ever took drugs. They might start treating you differently, like they did Debra, when they discovered her drinking problem. And let's ask them privately, not at breakfast or anything. Too many questions might be asked."

They found Noah and Shem outside of the kitchen, seemingly in a rather serious discussion. "Dad, can we talk to you. Cassie has some interesting spiritual questions. Not about *anyone* in particular, just things like: what if someone died that was a believer, but maybe not committed enough to act out his faith, before the Flood, things like that."

"Sure Japheth, but not now. You know I enjoy theological discussions. Even hypothetical ones usually have real-life applications. But just now we have a real problem, a big problem. We are running out of water. I'll be glad to talk to you later." Noah told them as he turned back to Shem.

They walked away. Cassie took his hand and said "Its Ok, Jay, opinions don't change facts, anyway. I'll ask Zalith. She's very knowledgeable in the spiritual area. Did you know that she attended the University?"

***

Cassie was now accustomed to spending her afternoons with Zalith. They talked about everything; they shared their experiences both before and on the Ark. Of course Zalith was very selective as to what she revealed about her past to Cassie, who was so entranced with Zalith's wardrobe that she rarely paid much attention to what Zalith was saying. Cassie loved the fabrics and workmanship. It reminded her of the days she spent with her mother. She would lovingly hold the familiar silks to her face, close her eyes and she was momentarily transported to her mother's workshop.

Something in Zalith's closet caught Cassie's attention. "Zalith, that's beautiful! Did you do that gorgeous embroidery? Can you teach me?" Cassia, since her family abstained from attending any type of religious event, was probably one of the few residents of Tymorrah that would not have immediately realized the significance of that embroidered robe.

"Haven't you ever seen a robe like this before? Maybe in town, at a ceremony or something?" Zalith cautiously asked.

Cassie, still admiring the intricate handiwork, absent-mindedly replied, "No. You know that I never would wear anything like this, but my mother taught me to appreciate good artistry. I would have remembered such a garment."

"Cassie, can you keep a secret?"

"Of course, but can't I even tell Jay?"

"No, no one, especially a man. They are just not capable of understanding some things. And what they can't understand, they try to destroy."

"But Jay is not like most men. He will understand and if he doesn't, he is just not the destroying type."

"Cassie, you have to promise me. Will you?"

"Well, OK, Zalith. If it's that important."

Zalith took Cassie's hand and quickly pricked one of her fingers with her embroidery needle. "Ouch! What was that for?"

"We need to make a covenant between us, and the mixing of our blood will bind us together as secret members of that covenant." Zalith said as she pricked her own finger. She placed her bleeding finger over

Cassia's and firmly squeezed them to extract more blood. Their blood dropped together onto a small ceramic plate that was on Zalith's worktable. Zalith tore a small piece of cotton fabric from one of the hand towels on her dresser. She daubed it into the small pool of congealing blood on the plate until the blood was totally absorbed into the fabric. She tore it in half, making sure that each piece had a spot of blood, and gave one of the pieces to Cassie.

"Never tell anyone about this and always wear this cloth, as a symbol of our covenant. But keep it concealed."

"Zalith, what are you talking about?"

"You just by-passed years of study and service to join the Sisterhood."

"Sisterhood?"

"I'll explain and teach you more everyday. But for starters, don't tell anyone. Just act as if we are only doing our hair and embroidering tablecloths. I am not the person that you and the others think that I am. I am a member of the Royal Family and a High Priestess of the Temple."

Cassie suddenly remembered the huntress in the forest. "Zalith, do you hunt?"

"Of course, all of the members of the Sisterhood were trained to hunt, and also in the arts of war."

When she saw the concerned look on Cassie's face, Zalith quickly tried to reassure her, "But I wouldn't hunt now. I just had to learn to join the priesthood."

Cassie was still suspicious, she had seen the look of triumph when Zalith killed the buck, but she didn't want to offend her friend. Not now. She would ask her later why hunting was so important. To her, hunting was cruel and useless; and she was positive that she would never join any group that required learning such a horrific skill.

"Cassie, don't you believe that all animals have spirits? Don't think of death as an ending, but as a beginning, a release of the spirit trapped in the body. A release that enables that spirit to enter a better realm, a totally spiritual realm."

"Do animals go to hell, Zalith"?

Zalith assumed an over-patient look as if she were dealing with a misinformed child, "No. There is no Hell. Forget everything that Noah and Shem taught you, even everything that Jay may have said in the area of religion. They are rather ignorant of the truth. Jehovah worship is so simplistic and exclusive. Every thing is either right or wrong to them.

Rather naïve, actually. The *real* spirit world is full of mystery, mysteries that are revealed to the faithful. Jehovah is just one of many spirits. Not at all the Creator and Upholder of the universe like Noah teaches. And there is no heaven and no hell."

"But Zalith, how can you be so sure?"

"I have communicated many times with the spirits of the dead. They are at peace, locked in an eternal spiritual union. Everything is made known to them. And death is the door to such a joyful world."

"Even to unbelievers, like my family? They didn't believe in the afterlife at all. Except maybe my brother, Thomas."

"Cassie, lets have a séance! You can see for yourself. Whatever spirit talks to us can tell you if there is a Hell or not. Tonight. We'll do it tonight. Tell Jay that you are working on a project with me and that we want to get it done as a present for his mother."

Cassie was becoming overwhelmed. She had expected only Zalith's opinions on the afterlife, not actual contact with the dead. "Zalith, I don't know. Can you actually talk to dead people?"

"Yes. I told you that I am not the weak and pathetically naïve person that I pretend to be. Ham doesn't even know the extent of my powers. He thinks that my worship is just a bunch of meaningless rituals. He thinks that they are cute and silly. I want to keep it that way, at least for now."

Chapter 28

The Ark, 2348 BC

Noah and Shem stared at the almost empty water reservoir.

"I never thought we would want for water. Remember when our initial water supply ran out and your mother figured out we could use the still her brother Tubal-cain gave her at our wedding? He gave it as a joke. He laughed about how she would need a large supply of alcohol after a few years of marriage to me. But Tubal-cain wasn't the only genius in that family; Naamah immediately saw its usefulness to purify water. But now the Ark is lodged on what appears to be a gigantic rock, and there is no water to draw up and purify, only an ever-thickening sea of mud. Mud too thick to use for water, but way too thin to support us to go and search for any."

"Father, what are we going to do? The animals drink more water every day, especially now that they are reproducing. The dogs just had their second litter born this morning, and all three of the cows have freshened. I never realized how much water an animal has to drink to make milk."

Noah remained silent for a few minutes and then replied, "Shem, this is beyond us. You, your brothers, and I need to spend the night in prayer and fasting. God is merciful. He would not bring us this far just to let us all die of thirst."

Chapter 29
Heaven: a council of the angels called by the Lord God

"Lucifer, from whence do you come?"

"The Ark. Where else? You have made the whole earth desolate. You see from Heaven how Noah is losing his faith. He hasn't slept for days worrying about their shrinking water supply, instead of depending on You. And he has been drinking and fantasying about his first wife, Emzara. His faith is superficial, my Lord. Not even he deserved Your salvation."

"You will never comprehend love or grace. You cannot understand compassion. You know only lies and evil. From now on you will no longer be called Lucifer, but Satan, the accusing one."

"Those lowly humans deserve my accusations! Even now, they have no faith in You. They doubt the ability of the earth to sustain them, they doubt Your mercy. They fear You will destroy the earth again, on a whim, that You toy with them."

"You, my created one, forget I know your motives. I see into your heart. I know you are trying to trick me into telling you the sign of my promise to Noah - so that you can reveal it to Zalith before the appointed time. You also forget that I know the future. I know what you cannot."

Satan, full of frustration and rebellion looked with hatred at the throne of God. He was blinded by the brightness of the radiant colors surrounding Him. He hissed and started to speak, but the Lord shut his mouth and returned him to earth.

If He created me, why does He let me persist? Maybe He can't destroy me. Maybe that "crush the head" prophecy was referring to someone else. But no – I am the most important and who else occupies the pages of His Word more than me? I can reason this out. Am I not the most intelligent being ever created? What would God use to symbolize his love and protection to those disgusting beings? What could He utilize throughout the ages as His Promise to never bring a Flood of total destruction to the earth again? He would desire to show a bridge spanning from heaven to earth. Yes! A physical reminder of His love and protection. Why does He love those creatures? Why did He ever make them? Ahh....because He loves me and wants to give me something to play with! He is playing a game with me!

Back to the symbol; concentrate. It must be majestic and heavenly, but explainable in an earthly fashion. I suspect it will have something to do with those blinding colors surrounding Him. I will hint of it, give Zalith enough information without being specific so whatever the sign is, she will know it is from me, or rather Inanna.

Chapter 30
The Ark, 2348 BC

"Jay, I won't be able to spend the evening with you tonight. Zalith and I have a project that we are working on, a present for your mother." Cassie didn't like lying to him and hoped Jay didn't notice how nervous she was.

"Actually, that's rather convenient because Dad asked Shem, Ham and me to spend the night in prayer with him. This way you will be busy, too. What about Debra, is she helping?"

"No. We didn't ask her. She's acting too weird. Why the prayer? Is there a problem?" *Of course I remember the water situation and please don't notice that I am twisting my hands! Please just go with your brothers. Go now! If you make me tell you what Zalith is planning, I know you won't like it and you'll go straight to your Dad and then Zalith will think I betrayed her.*

"Remember? Dad told us this morning that our water supply is running out. But don't worry. He'll think of something. He always does."

***

Noah was so deeply absorbed in his prayer that he hadn't noticed his sons had fallen asleep.

"Noah!"

"Yes Lord!" Noah replied as he immediately bowed to the ground, in thankful worship.

"You are my faithful and obedient servant. I will replenish the water daily, enough for you, your family and the animals. Each morning, at dawn, the tanks will be filled with fresh water."

"Thank you. My Lord, the God of my salvation."

Noah exhausted and overwhelmed with thankfulness and relief, relaxed and began to sleep while still in prayer. This was his first truly restful sleep in weeks; but it didn't last long. He awoke with the nagging feeling that something was wrong. He wasn't sure exactly what was bothering him, but there was some unrest, some problem that he needed to face.

Noah got up from the floor and went o his room. After he got into bed, he pulled Naamah close and told her God had answered his prayer; He would miraculously renew the water each morning. Together they offered a prayer of thanksgiving. Just before dawn, Noah suddenly awoke during a disturbing dream. *How odd, Lord was that from You?*

***

Zalith knew that she had to make the séance convincing, or she might lose her emotional grip on Cassie. *What if Cassie blew her cover? Would they burn her, stone her?* She smiled. *Probably not. It would be worse: an endless barrage of religious lectures, trying to reform me from my evil ways.*

She busied herself getting out her drapes, candles, robe, table cover, and crystal ball. I better not totally overwhelm her. I'll forgo the hat and statues for now. When her back was turned, she again heard a familiar voice calling to her. Her mother's smiling face appeared in the crystal ball.

"Zalith, what fun! A séance!"

"Oh Mother, can you appear to Cassie tonight?"

"Don't worry. Just proceed as usual. I will make sure Cassie is impressed. And there will be a special message, a promise for the future, for both of you."

Chapter 31
The Ark, 2348 BC

Cassie rubbed her finger where Zalith had pricked it this morning. *How very strange,* she mused. Cassie had long ago decided that her parents were wrong; the supernatural does exist. She had experienced the power of the spirits of the forest, even the rocks seemed to talk to her; especially when she was using the mind-expanding drugs her father provided for her. *I don't like the secrecy, and I don't like lying to my husband. Maybe I shouldn't go, but I don't want to disappoint Zalith. We've become such good friends and she seemed so excited.*

I'm getting excited; I wonder what it will be like? Sounds intriguing, but maybe it will just be tricks with lamps, mirrors and steam-propelled flying objects, like my father explained to me. He always said that the religious leaders played tricks on the worshippers to get them to give more money. Surely Zalith is not deceived by those kinds of tricks. And if she were planning only imitation spirits, why would she want to deceive me? I don't have anything to give her, only companionship. Her curiosity overcame her reluctance and she knocked on Zalith's door.

Zalith slowly opened the door, making sure that no one else was in the hallway. She grabbed Cassie's arm, pulled her into the room and quickly shut the door.

"Cassie, help me move this dresser in front of the door. We don't want any intruders."

Cassie was amazed at Zalith's strength, as she did most of the work moving the heavy oak dresser. *Now I'm trapped!* S*ecrecy usually means wrongdoing. Doesn't it?* She looked around at the dimly lit room, so different than it was a few hours ago. Candles were placed strategically, giving light, but also casting long ominous shadows and creating dark areas were the candles' light couldn't reach. The room smelled of some type of perfume. *What is that? I know that I have smelled that before. Oh yes, sandalwood incense. Some of the weavers who worked for my mother burned sandalwood incense to keep them focused when they were weaving especially intricate designs.* There was a round table in the center of the room, walled off by screens draped with dark curtains. The table was also covered with a heavy dark cloth. *Maybe my father was right. He said that fortunetellers and mystics used drapes and shadows to conceal their tricks.*

She noticed the crystal ball surrounded by three unlit candles: one white, one violet and one purple. Cassie had never seen colored candles before. *What a waste of good dye. Well that confirms it; Dad was right. He said never trust anyone with a crystal ball; a crystal ball only reveals reflected hidden images. Her father also said if spirits were real, they wouldn't need a big piece of glass to speak through. Is Ham behind the curtains, ready to respond to Zalith's cues? Magic tricks are harmless, anyway. Real ghosts could be scary.* She was somewhat relieved and decided to just enjoy the show.

Cassie sat down on the chair facing the door, but Zalith made her move to the other chair with her back to the door. Cassie relaxed even more. *It must just be magic tricks if the spirit's appearance depends on Zalith's location.*

Zalith sat down and covered her head with her square dark fringed shawl, made into a triangle by folding it in half. "Usually there are at least three people at a proper séance, but I'm sure that the spirits will understand. First we must make our own minds receptive. Breathe deeply and relax as much as possible. Try to empty your mind. Sometimes humming helps. Now we need to charge the candles. Hold each one in your hands, close your eyes and imagine the power of the spirits the candles represent."

When they were through with this visualization, Zalith lit the candles and returned them to their strategic places around the crystal ball. She took Cassie's hands and held them firmly in hers, making a ring around the crystal ball with their arms. Cassie could feel the warmth of the burning candles and began to worry about being trapped in a room full of wood on a ship made of wood if one of Zalith's long and loose sleeves began to burn.

"Cassie! You are thinking too much. Empty your mind of worldly things and worries."

Cassie tried to wipe all thought from her mind, but it wasn't working.

Zalith began to pray, "Oh Earth Mother, wise and beautiful One, bless this séance and allow one of your precious souls to visit the earth again. We desire that you allow the spirit world to open Cassia's mind to the truth."

"Cassie, close your eyes and breathe deeply and slowly: in through your nose and out through your mouth. Keep your mind blank." After a few minutes, Zalith began to summon the spirit of her mother.

"Our beloved Dehlia, the delight of Our Holy Goddess, commune with us, move among us. Cassie, repeat this with me until the spirit lets us know that she is here."

After about the sixth repetition of 'Our beloved Dehlia, the delight of Our Holy Goddess, commune with us, move among us', Cassie was becoming impatient.

"Zalith, this is getting boring."

"Shh…and keep your eyes closed. You need to be more respectful."

"Mother, if you are here, rap on the table three times!" Cassie was startled to hear the requested three raps, but still believed that Ham must be producing them by using a hammer and a pulley.

"Open your eyes now, Cassie, she is here."

Still skeptical and not knowing if she even wanted to see a spirit or not, Cassie opened her eyes.

"Mother, is Cassie's family there? Are they at peace? Rap once for 'yes' and twice for 'no'."

One rap. Then they heard a voice from above them.

"Ask Thomas himself" the voice of Dehlia told them.

"Mother! I knew you would come."

The center of the crystal ball began to glow. The small greenish glow enlarged and swirling images merged into a face in the center. Cassie was sure it was a trick with lamps and mirrors, but when the features emerged as those of her brother, she screamed.

"Cassie, don't mourn for us. We are happy and at peace." the image told her.

Cassie composed herself enough to ask about her parents. "And Mother and Father?"

"Yes," the ball responded. "All at peace."

Cassie's mind was spinning. *If even non-believers were rewarded with peace, what was the point of earthly obedience? Why was Zalith trying so hard to convince her if beliefs and actions on earth had no effect in the afterlife? And Thomas? He wasn't a goddess worshipper.*

Cassie had a moment of inspiration. "Thomas, what about our brothers and sisters, are they happy?"

"Yes, Cassie, and perhaps you can ask them yourself at some point."

"Even our baby sister, Althea."

"Yes, especially Althea, children are favored by the Goddess and hold a special place in her court. I must be returning now."

Cassie was overwhelmed with confusion. There was no baby sister, Althea. Cassie was the youngest. If that were Thomas, he would have known that. And Zalith described a peaceful totally spiritual existence, elevated above earthly matters. So what did the apparition mean when he referred to the goddess's court?

She didn't have time to reflect anymore. Something awesome was happening; the candles, their flames and the glowing crystal ball were all rapidly enlarging and merging into a lavender-colored cloud. The cloud rose above the table and began to swirl and elongate. The figure of a woman emerged. She was glowing. Her brilliance filled the room. She appeared to be smiling and benevolent, but powerful. Cassia could see that Zalith was just as surprised as she was at this obviously supernatural appearance.

"Cassie get on your knees and bow to Inanna."

Cassie didn't know what else to do, so she obeyed.

The figure spoke, "Arise my children. I have a message of great importance. I will send a magnificent sign to you. It will be so colorful, so feminine that you will immediately recognize it as from me. It will be a symbol of my existence and power throughout the ages. My followers will decorate their houses, their garments, and their windows for centuries to come. Of course, the Jehovah worshippers will claim it is from Him. Hold these words in your heart and keep them from the non-believers. We will know, just as in our rituals and prayers, that words and symbols can have dual meanings."

The image once again became a swirling cloud and then condensed into the crystal ball. Everything appeared as before except the candles were almost extinguished and burned down to table level.

"Zalith, it would have taken hours for the candles to burn this far down, maybe all night. Have we been here that long?"

"No, Cassie. Look at the other candles in the room. They are still mostly un-burned. It must be a sign for us, to know that She was really here or maybe the rapidly burning candles somehow let us visualize Her."

"Have you ever experienced anything as strange as that before?" Cassie asked

Zalith was visibly moved by the appearance of her Goddess. She was relaxed, but excited and strangely glowing and peaceful. "No, Cassie, wasn't it marvelous?"

Chapter 32
The Ark, 2348 BC

Debra was successful in her quest to lose track of time. She hadn't bathed, combed her hair, or changed her clothes for a while. *How long? A week or two at least, it doesn't really matter anyway.* She tried to keep up with her animal duties. They needed her and at least they were always glad to see her. To avoid seeing Shem, actually to avoid all of them, she tried to do all of her chores early, slipping back to her room before breakfast. Naamah brought her food and put clean water in her washbasin. She always made sure she had clean linen and towels. Instead of being grateful, Debra was starting to resent Naamah and was glad that she usually came to her room while she was working.

"Is she trying to hint that I need to wash? How many clean towels does one person need?" Debra quizzed the cattle. They didn't seem to care how unkempt she was. She moved on to her favorite, the sheep. "Blackie, do you realize that you guys are the only thing keeping me sane?"

She went to the water tanks to get them fresh water. On the way, she slipped on some seaweed and decomposing fish that one of the men had left in a pile on the deck. *Men! Why can't they clean up their own messes? I'll come back later and do it when I get done watering.* She was seething. *I could have broken my neck! I could have hit the railing, lost my balance, and fallen overboard into that sea of mud, ick! No one could swim in that. The animal waste and dirty straw just sink quietly now, not even making a splash when thrown overboard or pushed out of the vents on the lower decks.*

When Debra returned with her load of water, Naamah was looking for her.

"Hi, Debra. Can we talk? I'm getting very worried about you."

"Mother Naamah, I'm fine. I am not in the mood for a lecture. Besides, I don't have time, there's a big mess on the deck that I need to clean.

"Well, what I have to say won't take long. I'll help with the milking. And you are wrong; you're not fine. Look at you. Your eyes are sinking into your head because you are getting so thin, your hair is dirty and unkempt, and your clothes are stained. No one wants to be around you. Frankly, dear, you are getting smelly and nobody knows what to say to you. Where is the meticulous and thoughtful woman that got on this boat? If you are the victim in this situation, why are you the only one suffering? Angry self-pity will just burn inside of you, eating you away. Debra, you can't depend on someone else for your happiness. You have to take responsibility for your own spiritual relationship with God, and then everything else will eventually work itself out. Try to forgive Shem, no matter what, and get on with your lives. Don't you want a family? Don't you want children?" asked Naamah as she picked up her milk buckets to take them to the kitchen.

"I won't lecture you anymore, but think about it."

***

Zalith, armed with increased spiritual strength from a personal visit from Inanna, decided that it was time to finally remove that extreme annoyance, Debra. Not only would her murder remove the possibility of the foretold Redeemer, but also Inanna would gladly accept such a sacrifice. There wouldn't be the customary ceremonies, but those were mainly for the crowd, anyway. She was confident that her goddess would understand that under the circumstances, she was doing her best.

She took one of her personal wine casks from her room and poured two cups. Although the cups had the same ceramic style, they were different colors to make sure she wouldn't get them confused, and drink the poison herself. *I bet Debra can't refuse this wine, even if she refuses to talk to me.* She tried to make the tray as inviting as possible and added the sleeping powder to the cup she intended to be Debra's.

On the way to the storage room where Debra was staying, she met Naamah. *This probably looks suspicious, even to poor dumb Naamah. But at least she can be a witness of my good intentions.*

"Do you know where Debra is? I want to try and make peace with her. I know that she is angry with me, and I want to apologize, even though I don't really know what I am apologizing for," Zalith said, smiling sweetly.

"Well, whatever the problem is between you two, I am all for mending it. Debra said something about cleaning up a mess on the deck. But I don't know if this is a good time to talk to her, and do you think that wine is a good choice for Debra? You know that she has a problem with wine."

"Its OK, it's diluted with water, honey and spices so much that there is hardly any wine at all," Zalith told her, knowing that her private store of wine was at least twice as strong as that which Naamah served at dinner.

"Well it will be good for her to know that you are concerned, I suppose. Good luck."

***

Naamah watched Zalith leave. *Why do I feel so uneasy? She only wants to apologize, I think – why else would she bring Debra a drink in a pretty cup? But that's a lie that you don't know why she is upset with you. Debra told me she saw you kissing her husband. At least I am presuming it was you. Maybe you really do want to reassure Debra; or maybe the whole thing didn't even happen except in Debra's imagination. I hope your innocence isn't in my imagination.*

***

Zalith found Debra busily cleaning the slippery and smelly mess. *How ridiculous she looks, down on her knees with her skirts tied to her waist and her hair a tangled dirty mess. Maybe she isn't a worthy sacrifice after all. But at least she is conveniently already on the deck.*

"Debra, I brought…"

Debra was so absorbed in her cleaning that she jumped at the sound of Zalith's voice.

"Go away. I want nothing to do with you and I have nothing to say to you."

"Please," Zalith pleaded. "I want to make things right between us. I brought us some wine to drink. This is excellent wine, very dry and heady, Ham and I purchased it in Tymorrah before we left."

"I don't want to drink with you. I don't even want to talk to you."

"Alright. I will just leave it here for you."

"I don't want it. Take it with you."

"But Debra…it's really good…"

"I can't believe that you would have the nerve to talk to me! If everyone thinks I am a drunk how dare you bring me 'heady wine' to tempt me. Leave me alone."

Zalith started to put the tray down but Debra angrily hit it with the back of her hand as Zalith bent down to place it beside her. The tray tipped forward, spilling the contents of the cups down Debra's dress, adding more spots to her already stained clothes.

Zalith patiently sighed, "I was only trying to make you feel better. Let me know when you're ready to talk."

Zalith left, but only went far enough to feel confident that Debra's back was once again facing away from her, and that she was busy cleaning on her hands and knees. *She couldn't have made it easy, could she?*

Zalith removed the dagger that she always had strapped to her right thigh from its leather scabbard, and quickly turned back to Debra, intending to grab her by the hair and slit her throat.

***

Debra saw Zalith's shadow moving rapidly towards her, and turned around just in time to avoid the attack. Zalith's momentum carried her forward into Debra, knocking Debra onto her back with Zalith on top of her. The dagger lodged in one of the wooden planks above their heads.

Even though Debra had never been in any type of physical battle before, she was in top condition from the long days of hard work on the Ark, while Zalith had barely lifted a finger for almost a year. Debra, now with superior weight and strength, as well as the advantage of her dress already being tied around her waist, giving her better use of her legs, was able to turn them both over. She grabbed Zalith's left arm and used her legs to twist them so that Zalith was now on her back. Debra straddled Zalith's body, whose own well-trained legs were useless, entangled in her long tight skirt.

"Help! Ham! Noah! She is trying to kill me!" Zalith screamed.

"What? You attacked me!"

"You know no one will believe you. You're the crazy one."

Zalith once more tried to extract herself from Debra's knee-grip. She squirmed upward and tried to reach for the dagger, but Debra's longer arms were able to extract it from the plank first. Debra pulled it above her head, out of Zalith's reach.

"Now every one will know how evil you are. They'll believe me!"

"Debra, don't you want to die? It would do you and all of us a lot of good." Zalith said, mustering enough strength to be sarcastic.

"Why do you want to kill me? Do you want my husband that badly?"

"No, life on earth will just be better without you. I will get Shem eventually anyway."

That remark was too much for Debra. She angrily screamed, "No! You will never have him!"

Shem was the first to view the scene of Debra holding a knife above Zalith and proclaiming, "you will never have him!"

Shem quickly grabbed Debra's wrist and squeezed. "Drop it!"

He roughly pulled her up, "Debra, if I hadn't seen it with my own eyes, I wouldn't have believed it; I would have never believed that you were capable of murder."

"And you have been drinking again." His expression reflected his disgust as he looked at her dirty and stained dress, reeking of wine and long-dead fish.

Chapter 33
The Ark, 2348 BC

The others soon arrived Ham looked at Zalith, "What happened?"

"Ham, I don't know. She tried to kill me!"

Ham sprung at Debra. Shem turned her away and Ham lunged forward onto the railing. He started to turn back to strike Shem and then stopped when he saw the dagger. He had seen its golden jeweled handle often enough to know to whom it belonged.

"Zalith, go back to our room. I will be there soon to talk to you," Ham said with unaccustomed firmness. He looked at Zalith, Shem and Debra and suddenly everything was clear to him: Zalith and Shem were having an affair and that was the source of Debra's anger, insanity and drinking.

"Yes. Please, Zalith, go so we can get to the bottom of this," Noah told her.

"Naamah, please take Debra to one of the empty storage rooms and lock it somehow from the outside. Attempted murder is a very serious charge."

***

Ham angrily burst into their bedroom. Before Zalith could speak, Ham backhanded her on the face, sending her reeling across the room. Fortunately, she landed with her back facing him, so that he could not see the hard glare of hatred in her eyes. Zalith rubbed her face and said to herself, *someday he will pay for that, pay dearly, but for now I need him on my side*. She quickly composed herself and let the tears from the pain and shock that someone would dare to hit her, run down her face.

Ham rushed to her side, "Zalith, I am so sorry! I didn't mean to hurt you! I love you so much that the thought of you with another man makes me crazy. Especially my brother! What happened? Why did you try to kill Debra? We both know that it was your dagger."

"Ham, I admit that I have been flirting with Shem. Remember that I told you that I know how to control him? But it never went beyond that. Debra just assumed that it did. I went to talk to her, to explain that nothing was going on between Shem and me. She just became angrier, grabbed me by the leg and pulled me down. Then she saw the dagger and pulled it from the scabbard. I think she would have done me in, really, if you and the others hadn't come to my rescue."

"Zalith, I want to believe you. You know that I love you, but somehow all the pieces aren't fitting together. Please, just be good; stop your damned goddess-worship, so you don't give anyone any ammunition against you."

Zalith was silent; her head down, seemingly reflecting on what Ham had said. Actually, she was receiving a revelation from her personal spirit guide. She told her to agree. Hide the truth for a while, maybe a long while, until the right moment was revealed.

"Yes Ham, you're right. From now on, I will be the perfect wife and obedient to your parents' ways. Almost dying has instantaneously changed me. Whatever doubts I had before about your father's religion are gone, erased. I don't want to go to Hell, really. And Ham, you know my life before we were married. This one man for one woman is strange to me. But I was only flirting; I never meant it to progress. Please believe me, I love you so much, I wouldn't want anything to come between us."

Ham held her tightly. "Honey I'm sorry if I seem skeptical. Its just that I know you're such a good actress."

Her face, bruised and hidden in his shoulder became hardened again and she silently vowed to some day have revenge. *How dare he hit me*!

Chapter 34

The Ark, 2348 BC

Cassie and Japheth walked away in stunned silence, leaving Noah and Shem alone. Neither one spoke for what seemed an eternity. Shem was devastated by what he had just seen: partly because of what he presumed to be Debra's actions, but mainly because of the guilt of knowing that she was reacting to what she presumed to be his unfaithfulness.

"Shem, apparently I don't know my daughters-in-law very well, but I think that I know my sons. I also know that Lucifer attacks those that threaten him the most. Think about it, before the Flood, he had millions of people to torment and tempt. Now there are only eight of us. I know that there are doubts and questions in my mind that were never there before. Even your Mother, from whom I haven't heard a complaint in over one hundred years, has told me she has lately been feeling discontented and neglected. Lucifer loves to amplify doubt and discontent. Don't you think that perhaps he is ultimately at the bottom of this quarrel between Debra and Zalith?"

"I don't know Dad, I blame myself."

"That's just what I mean! Feelings of guilt and self-doubt ruin lives and relationships. They paralyze a person's actions, so much so that nothing ever gets accomplished. Those feelings aren't from God. God wants us to face our transgressions, confess them, ask forgiveness and accept that forgiveness when it is given. Then move on. The Liar wants us to wallow in doubt, guilt and self-pity."

Shem continued his silence, but things were beginning to make a little sense to him. *If Zalith arranged it to make him look bad to Debra, could she have arranged that whole scene to make Debra appear the villain? Perhaps Zalith is a goddess-worshipper and was wearing the priestess robes, just like Debra said. Maybe I was wrong and it wasn't Debra's imagination. I should have just believed her in the first place. Whether Lucifer or Zalith are the cause of all this strife I don't know, but perhaps it doesn't matter, at the moment they seem one and the same.*

"When God told me to build the Ark and to warn the others about the impending Flood, I only thought about their immediate physical salvation, not their actual eternal salvation. I suppose I believed that if they joined us, that was enough. They would believe when the Flood happened, just as God said that it would. When the three of you married,

I believed the women were hand picked by God. But maybe I was wrong. I never worried about insuring that their spiritual lives were in line with ours. I was just too busy or assumed too much." He paused for a while, and then asked, "What happened to your scripture studies? Why did you stop them?"

"I'm not sure. I didn't feel that I was worthy enough to tell anyone how to act."

"Another one of the Devil's lies. Shem, none of us are perfect. You can't expect yourself to be perfect; you are only heading for defeat. Besides, your job is to talk about God's perfection, grace and love - not yours. Look at me, God knows me. He knows that I am not perfect, yet He chose me to build the Ark to save the animals as well as us. Don't you think that He could have easily re-created a different world?

But being human also means being able to choose or reject God. God created us to be able to choose, because true love, the love that God desires from us, can't be demanded, only freely given; and being human, sometimes we make bad choices. We need help. Remember in the Garden, God promised a Savior for us. Remember, 'the Seed of the woman will crush the head of the Serpent'? We know that means one of Eve's descendents will deal a fatal blow to the Devil."

"Yes, but what does that have to do with us now?"

"Well, Shem, like I said, I think that I know my sons and I think that I know from which line that Savior will come. Japheth is kind and gentle. He would do whatever I asked him, but he is not spiritually healthy and I can't say exactly why. I know he is struggling because he loved God's destroyed creation, even more than the One who created it. He resents God's judgment. He hasn't totally submitted himself to God and maybe he never will. Ham seems to have little spiritual discernment. His self-interest may keep him from ever being a true believer. That leaves you. You can't procreate by yourself. Get things right with Debra."

"But, Dad, I can't. I don't know how."

"First we need to make sure that Debra is on the correct spiritual path, then we, or rather you, can start to mend your relationship." He turned his back to Shem and was silent for a time.

Shem thought that his father was going to leave, but then Noah turned back to him and began to speak, "When I was a young man, I remember my father and Methuselah talking about a ceremony they preformed when a person outside the faith wanted to convert, or a person wanted to make a special commitment. We need to instruct your wife and sisters-in-law, and then have a public water purification ceremony. It had a specific name, it was called mmmm…? I'll think of it in a minute."

"What's that, what type of ceremony? And I agree that they might need some spiritual instruction, but I don't think that I am the one to do it. They wouldn't listen to me, not now."

"Don't worry, I will ask your mother to instruct them, and as I remember, the ceremony is a proclamation of faith and then an emersion into water to symbolize a change in the new believer. To tell you the truth, I have never seen it. We haven't had a conversion for a long time. But Methuselah said that when the one undergoing the ritual is under the water it is as if they are dead, without God. When they come up out of the water they are alive, one of God's own."

"Dad isn't that a little silly? I mean water can't really change them, can it?"

"No. It's a bit of a mystery, but Methuselah said that it was very important to solidify their new commitment, to make it public. Oh, wait a minute. Now I remember: it was called Mikvah. Of course God knows who has really made a spiritual commitment to Him and who has not. To those that have, the water becomes almost living. It renews and strengthens them; it symbolizes the washing away of their old life. It is symbolic of their purification before God. To those that have not really changed, it is just a dunk in the water."

"Does it forgive their sins?"

"Of course not, only God can do that. We ask for forgiveness through confession and sacrifice."

Suddenly Shem's face went pale. "Dad, do you mean that if Debra and I don't make up, millions of souls will be lost? I don't know that I can handle that much responsibility."

Noah smiled, "Just take it day by day. Nothing that any of us do can interfere with God's plans for a Savior. Yes, we do make choices that affect the future, but God is beyond time and He knows the future. His promises will be fulfilled. He knows our choices before we do. It's something that we can't really understand. His ways are beyond our understanding. Fortunately, they are also beyond the Devil's understanding. He is only a created being and not the equal of the Almighty. Just remember, God loves you. Put your faith in His promises. I could be wrong about you fathering the Redeemer's line. I mean, look at your mother's family: brilliant but violent, and in total rebellion against God. Yet your mother was able to overcome that influence and become the godly woman that we know. God knows what He is doing, and He won't ask the impossible from you."

Noah embraced his son and started to walk away. As he was leaving he said, "I am going to a have a talk with Debra. I'll see you at dinner, if you have time to eat. You will need to perform Debra's duties as well as yours, at least until I can figure things out."

Suddenly Noah stopped and turned back to Shem. "Shem! Wait! I just remembered a dream that I had. I can't believe that I almost forgot it; it was such a strange dream. *Now* I know what it meant, at least partially."

Shem turned back expectantly to his father. He didn't usually rely very much on the meaning of dreams, but he trusted his father to know what was important and possibly prophetic. At the moment, he was eager for any insight. "What?"

"We were standing on a beach. You, your brothers and I were talking and laughing on a little knoll. The women were a little closer to the water, combing and braiding each other's hair, I think. I am not exactly sure what they were doing, but everyone was in a jovial mood. Then a beautiful little bird came up to us. It was a delightful bright blue, with a pale yellow head. It seemed to have an almost human intelligence as it flew about, landing on our shoulders and serenading us with an enchanting, melodious song. It landed first on Ham's shoulder, then yours and finally mine. I don't think it went to Japheth. Anyway, from my shoulder, it looked over at the women. It started to fly towards them, and it began to change. It grew larger, started shrieking instead of singing and its color turned from a light blue to a dark and iridescent hue. I remember the sunlight hitting the feathers and them changing from dark blue to green and then back to blue. It was strange that I noticed because I don't normally think much about the colors of a bird's feathers. The colors must be significant somehow, but that significance eludes me right now. Anyway, it began to viscously attack Debra, tearing at her flesh with its beak and claws. She was screaming for us to help her, but we didn't respond. We didn't even take one-step in her direction. Naamah and Cassie walked away, deep in conversation, out of my view and..."

Shem interrupted, "Dad, you said Mom and Cassie, where was Zalith?"

"That's right; I do remember only your mother and Cassie. Maybe Zalith wasn't in the dream, I guess, I don't remember now. The four of us turned our backs and began to talk louder so we couldn't hear her. At one point you asked Debra to please control herself, it was only a pretty little bird. I was relieved when the screaming stopped; it was tearing at my soul, but I couldn't move to help her. I turned to see Debra's lifeless and bleeding body lying on the sand. The bird started to fly back to us, and as it did, it once again turned into its former beautiful self. It landed on my shoulder, began to sing and then flew to you. I looked at my shirt where the bird had been perched and noticed with horror its bloody claw prints. I was stricken with guilt and began to cry. Then I woke up"

"What do you think the dream meant?"

"That something is attacking Debra, and we are not helping her: maybe a spiritual attack, maybe physical, I am not sure. But I'm sure God sent that dream to prepare me for what just happened. It is clearly telling me things are not always what they appear to be." Noah started to walk away again.

"I really do need to talk to both of them."

Shem also turned away. He had a lot of work to do, but even more to think about. He knew exactly what that dream meant and whom that bird represented. He needed to somehow make things right with Debra, but even more importantly, he needed to protect her.

Chapter 35

The Ark, 2348 BC

Zalith reassured Ham that she was all right and that it was OK for him to go back to work. "Really Ham; I need some time to think about my new commitment. I need some time alone to spend in prayer."

Ham gently kissed her goodbye and left. He noticed with a pang of guilt the bruise starting to darken her face where he struck her. He still wasn't convinced of her conversion, but at least he hoped that she was intending to at least pretend to change. *I suppose it doesn't really matter what she believes, as long as it appears like she follows my parents. I am not a believer either, at least not the way my parents and Shem are, and things seem to be just fine with me. At least Zalith and I are both alive.*

***

After Ham left, Zalith quickly ran to the storage area, hoping to eavesdrop on any conversation that Debra was having. She couldn't wait to hear what Noah said to Debra about the attack. She presumed that Debra was in the room with the large trunk in front of it so she slipped into the next room and curled up close to the adjoining wall. She was still toying with the idea of sacrificing Debra and making the murder look like suicide.

Naamah certainly didn't think that trunk would keep anyone in or out of that room. The door opened in, all I would have to do is climb on top of it, sneak into the room, stab her in the chest while she sleeps, and put the knife in her hand. Maybe I should suffocate her first with a pillow or something. That would guarantee the knife placement, no extraneous wounds to indicate they weren't self-inflicted.

***

Noah also found Debra's temporary jail by the large trunk that had been put in front of the door. "Debra, can I come in?"

Debra had been waiting for Noah, but she wasn't expecting the gentle and concerned tone in his voice. Sitting alone, she thought about the afternoon's events and realized what the scene must have looked like to them. She wasn't expecting anyone to be on her side. She even had to admit that if she were in their place she would be making the same assumptions. She was beginning to feel that Zalith was right, life would be better for everyone else if she were dead.

"Yes, please."

Noah pushed the trunk away and opened the door. Then he closed it after him. "Debra, I feel that I need to apologize to you. I didn't mean to ignore your obvious pain, when I did notice that something wasn't right with you, I assumed that Shem and Naamah could handle it."

Debra was still amazed at the kindness in his voice. "Father Noah, it's not your fault. Zalith and Shem are responsible, not you."

"I have a slightly different theory; I believe that the Devil is the ultimate villain, and that if I had taken the responsibility to instruct you girls more seriously, you could have withstood The Liar better."

"No! Its all Zalith's doing."

"Tell me what happened."

"First, the morning that you all found me in the wine room, I wasn't drunk. I had been…"

"I suspected that you weren't, and again I apologize, that was my empty cask and I meant to throw it away later. I had forgotten about it. I never should have let them blame you, but you did look rather inebriated. I sometimes have some extra wine and I supposed that maybe you did too, the wine helps me relax and forget."

He smiled, "saving the world is a big job, you know."

Then he became serious again, "But it also helps me deal with some of my grief. You and I have that in common; we both lost loved ones in the deluge. I heard people calling your name through the din, as well as mine. Shem told me that for months you had nightmares about it. You know we tried; we really tried to save your family. They just wouldn't listen. I remember at the wedding, I overheard your father talking to your uncle about what a good match you made. They approved because I was rich and wouldn't live forever. I interrupted them. It seemed a good opportunity to talk about eternal life, to remind them that none of us would live forever. They just laughed and drank some more of my wine. Debra, you can grieve, but don't feel responsible; they were warned. It's difficult, I know. I do feel responsible for the loss of my family, my ex-wife and our…. did you know that I was married before and had eight other children? I never mentioned it to the boys, I don't know exactly why."

"Yes, I know." Debra stopped; she didn't want to betray Naamah's trust.

Noah went on, "Yes, I think everyone in Tymorrah knew my wife and children left me because they thought I was crazy. You know, being right doesn't ease the pain very much. I should have been able to convince them, and now they are lost. I don't want to lose my new daughters as well."

"But Father Noah, I know my family didn't believe. I was starting to accept that they were destroyed because of their evil practices. When I saw Zalith doing the same thing, I was resentful that my family was destroyed and she still lived. Why did God allow her to be saved? Shem didn't even believe me; he thought the wine and my grief made me imagine it."

***

Noah decided that they were becoming sidetracked and decided to ask the big question that he needed Debra to answer, "Debra, did you try to kill her?"

"No, she attacked me. I was only holding the knife out of her reach until someone came to help."

Noah was reluctant to cast blame on either of his daughters-in-law. He didn't know what had made Debra accuse Zalith of participating in evil activities. He would investigate that later. "I don't want either of you to ever be alone the rest of our journey. I want to prevent you from hurting yourself or anyone else, or anyone or anything hurting you. I am convinced that Lucifer or his demons are influencing both of your actions. I am going to take you to be with Naamah while I go talk to Zalith, but will you pray with me?"

Noah asked God to re-new her spirit and to protect her from whatever physical or spiritual attack she was experiencing.

***

Debra was grateful that Noah, although he didn't know all the details of her distress, seemed to be very concerned for her; concerned enough to pray for her. The past year had revealed with certainty that God had a special love for Noah. If anyone could intercede for her emotional, physical and spiritual healing, it would be Noah.

Something inexplicable was happening to her as she walked with him to the kitchen. With every step, she felt more and more relaxed. There was a peace in her soul that she had never experienced before. At first, she thought the feeling was a response to Noah and his love and kindness, but by the time they reached the kitchen, she realized this was beyond human; her inner peace was a reassurance from God.

Chapter 36
The Ark, 2348 BC

After Zalith heard Noah and Debra leave, she bolted back to her room before Noah arrived. It had been difficult to stay silent and not start laughing while listening to Debra's complaints and Noah's silly dribble. *But why didn't Noah at least reprimand her? What about the angry accusations I was expecting to enjoy? At least I know what my defense will be, if it comes to that. I just need to pretend some type of demonic influence. Imagine that they believe in such things!* She laughed, and then tried to look distraught as she sat on her bed and waited for Noah's knock on her door.

***

Naamah was confused and a little apprehensive when Noah brought the dirty and tear-stained Debra to her in the kitchen.

"Noah! Do you think this is a good idea?" Naamah said to him as she pointedly looked at the kitchen knives.

"I'll explain later. I don't think Debra should be alone and I need to talk to Zalith."

"It's OK, Noah. We'll be fine." Naamah replied calmly but was trying to envision what kitchen tasks Debra could do that didn't involve any sharp utensils.

"Debra, remember that you are not to be alone at anytime." Noah walked out the door but quickly returned, "And maybe you can use the time before dinner to get cleaned up."

"Well dear, you are looking remarkably well, I am happy to say. That distraught look is gone and I see a smile lurking. Do you feel like talking? Come over here and help me fold these towels and fill me in on the details. I'll heat some water for you to freshen up a bit."

***

As Noah approached Zalith's door, he hesitated. The closer he got to her door, the more uncomfortable he became. *Perhaps I should have Ham present: that would be best.* He wasn't sure of the source of his reluctance to be around Zalith, at least to be around her alone, but after the day's events and that unsettling dream, he thought he should trust his instincts.

Ham was coming up the hall. "Good that you are here son, I want to talk to Zalith and I want you to be there."

"Surely you believe that Zalith is totally innocent? She would never try to harm anyone."

"Debra says that Zalith attacked her. Would she have any reason to do so, that you know of?"

"No", Ham said emphatically.

Zalith hearing them talking, opened the door. She threw her arms around Ham's neck.

"Thank goodness you are here. I don't want to be alone, ever. I feel like the shadows are talking to me, and even trying to hurt me."

Noah gently told her to go back into the room and tell him what happened.

"Dad, I know what happened, Debra attacked her, she's crazy"

"No, Ham, I lied to you." Zalith said matter-of-factly.

"Just let me explain. I need to tell you both the truth. I went to Debra to try and make things right between us; the tension was wearing on me. I made us some wine punch and took it up to where Naamah said Debra was working, but she didn't want to talk to me. When I tried to leave the punch for her, she angrily spilled it. I turned to leave and then suddenly…well I am not sure what happened, it was like I didn't have control of myself."

"Just as I suspected, go on Zalith." Noah interrupted.

"When I lived in Tymorrah, my mother gave me a dagger to always wear for self-defense. I am not sure why I still wear it. You know that I am deathly afraid of animals, maybe I just wanted to be ready if one attacked me; or maybe it just reminds me of my mother. Anyway, I started to walk away and then, almost against my own will, I pulled out the dagger and rushed towards Debra. After that, I am not sure what happened. Thank goodness she is stronger then I am, so I wasn't able to really hurt her." Zalith covered her face with her hands and began to sob.

"There, there dear. Please try to compose yourself, we need to get this thing straightened out." Noah awkwardly patted her shoulder. *Why is Ham just standing there with his mouth open and saying nothing? He could at least try to comfort her.*

"At least one good thing happened, when I thought that Debra might actually kill me, I realized that I didn't want to go to Hell, and that if I survived, I would make sure that I had a correct relationship with God."

"Then you will welcome my idea. I want you and the other two girls to seriously study God's Word and God's attributes, then publicly declare your new faith."

"Whatever you think is best, Father Noah."

"And I don't want you to be alone."

Noah left. As he walked back to the kitchen he thought, *well that was easy, maybe a little too easy. I wonder where she really got that knife? That gold-handled jeweled dagger wasn't from a poor family that needed to sell their precious daughter into prostitution. Her father would have made as much money selling the dagger, as he would have from selling Zalith to the temple authorities.*

***

Ham continued his silence. Just as he suspected, Zalith had initiated the attack. He turned his back to Zalith so he could think without her interrupting his thoughts. *I am sure this newly found piety is an act.* He smiled. *It seems much more in character for her to be angry with Debra and to attack her than to let herself be helplessly taken over by some mysterious force.* He wondered what punishment his wife would receive. He also wondered if anyone would realize that he, and not Debra had caused the bruise on her face.

Chapter 37

The Ark, 2348 BC

Shem prayed while he worked. He asked God to bring him wisdom and understanding when he talked to Debra. He also asked that Debra find it in her heart to forgive him. At last, he felt a calming reassurance, an answer to his prayer. He knew everything would be all right.

When he was finished with the double load of chores, he rushed to the storage area to talk to Debra. With horror he saw the trunk pushed away and the door open. He panicked. Where was she? He forgot the peace of mind that had reassured him when he was praying. All manner of horrible scenarios were racing through his mind, foremost among them was that Debra escaped to do herself in. *In her state of mind suicide would seem an easy way out.* He rushed to the kitchen to ask his mother if she knew where Debra was. When he saw Debra, he forgot his pride and carefully planned speech. He rushed to her, took her in his arms and held her tightly.

"Debra, I thought I had lost you forever!" Shem said while he stroked Debra's dirty and tangled hair.

Naamah was smiling so much she could barely speak, "Why don't you two skip dinner and go talk things out. I'll pack you something to take with you. Debra, remember Noah doesn't want you to be alone."

"I'll see to that, Mother. Gladly."

Shem took the cheese, bread and dried fruit from his mother and led Debra down the hall. "You need to sleep in our room tonight; you'll be safer there. Don't worry; I'll sleep on the floor."

"Shem, what happened? Why are you being so nice to me? Why so protective?"

"I know now that your were right about Zalith all along. I should have believed you in the first place. I don't know exactly what happened today, but I do know that she would harm you if given the chance. Dad thinks she is demon-possessed or something. I think she is just evil."

***

Hearing Shem call Zalith evil was music to Debra's ears. She felt as if a two-ton weight was lifted from her shoulders. "Your Dad talked to me. I was expecting condemnation and punishment. He surprised me by being so loving and kind. He even apologized for neglecting me. He prayed with me, or rather for me. Not just a routine repetition of words, like we sometimes do at dinner, but a heartfelt prayer asking God to renew and protect me."

"Dad wants to make sure the three of you are instructed properly in the basics of Jehovah worship and then have you declare your faith in a public cleansing ceremony."

She wasn't sure how to reply. As she ate, Debra realized how hungry she really was. She felt like she hadn't eaten in days and for all she knew, she hadn't. The last few weeks were such a blur.

"Shem, I do so desperately want to feel free from my old self. Let's do that ceremony now."

"What?"

"The ceremony. I need it now. I need a new beginning. We need a new beginning. Besides, if Noah wants me ceremonially cleansed with Zalith present, or worse, together, I don't know that I can."

"But Debra, I don't know how. I've never seen it"

"I have. They always purified the adult sacrifices to make sure they were worthy of being sacrificed. Many times those being sacrificed were very willing; they wanted to free their spirits, or earn their rewards, or something. Other times worshippers would be ceremonially washed who just wanted to publicly display their commitment. From what I remember and what I've learned, everything the Temple leaders did was either in direct opposition to, or a twisted imitation of God's instructions to the faithful."

"I don't know…Well, I guess we can use one of the water storage tanks," Shem reluctantly agreed.

"Besides, I could use a good bath" Debra replied as she took clean clothes, towels and a hairbrush from her dresser. She caressed the polished and well-worn wood like a long-lost lover.

She smiled, "Fortunately God renews the water supplies every morning. Lets go."

It was a beautiful moonlit night. The reflection of the moon and stars on the rippling water made the water tank appear to be a sea of dancing lights. Debra quickly stripped down to her under slip and climbed into the tank.

"C'mon, Shem the water is wonderfully warm."

Shem was finding it difficult to concentrate on spiritual matters. All he could think about was Debra's almost naked and graceful body swimming around below him. He stripped down to his trousers and slowly let himself down into the sun-warmed water.

"All right, now what?"

"Try to think of a sentence or two that describes our faith; something that will affiliate me with Jehovah, and no other god, if I agree to your statements."

Aroused, Shem had to turn his back to her so he could think. When he composed what he supposed were the appropriate questions, he turned back to her. "Debra do you agree that there is only one true Living God, the Creator and Sustainer of the universe?"

"Yes"

"Do you agree to put no other gods before Him, to put away all idols and to follow His laws?"

"Yes"

Before Shem could help her, Debra dove under the water. When she arose, Shem declared that she was now a member of the family of Jehovah.

"Shem, do you know what I feel like?"

"No, but I do know you've had quite an eventful day."

"Yes! I started out as an outcast and progressed to a suspected criminal. Then your father helped me to realize that not only him but also God cares for me. And your mother! I never let her know how much her concern meant to me. Even on my worse days, she tried to get me back on track, and her words of wisdom helped me come out of my cocoon of pain and self-pity. Cocoon! That is exactly how I feel; like a butterfly that has gone from a worm to a hidden, dissolved goo in a cocoon, and finally to a beautiful winged creature. I feel like I have been given a new life, a new beginning."

Shem had to admit, there was a noticeable transformation in Debra, physically, spiritually and mentally.

She swam closer to him, put her arms around his neck and kissed him full on the mouth. "You don't have to sleep on the floor tonight," she warmly told him.

Then she backed away and laughingly splashed his ever-serious face, "But if you call me Zalith, I will have to find that dagger."

She climbed out of the water tank and gathered up her belongings.

Shem was shocked that she could joke about such things, but followed her lead as she ran, sopping wet, back to their room.

Chapter 38
The Ark, Friday, September 4th, 2348 BC

Cassie was thankful for the spiritual lessons; it gave her time to think and balance the things Naamah was teaching against Zalith's instructions. She wasn't as gullible as Zalith thought. Her father had raised her to be a skeptic, especially in the area of religion.

It was a beautiful sunny morning as she sat in the aviary intently discussing her spiritual quandary with her special pet dove, Josie.

"Well, Josie, help me decide. Who do I believe? Zalith says I can believe both, as long as I don't worship Jehovah exclusively. Naamah says Jehovah demands that all other gods be forsaken. Zalith has to worship in secret. She says that's OK; secrecy makes religion more exciting, but I just don't trust something that has to be hidden. She tells me her conversion isn't totally faked, meaning she always believed that Jehovah existed. I know that Naamah's Jehovah is not the same as Zalith's. To believe Zalith is to deny Naamah's God, as the one true God. Zalith says our water purification will mean nothing. It's just to reassure Noah. Naamah says that it is a serious matter and we shouldn't do it if we are unsure. Zalith has no intention of abandoning her goddess, but intends to go through the ceremony anyway."

She twirled around with Josie on her finger. She laughed as she noticed her little friend's eye's bobbing. "Get your bearings Josie, you need to help me think this out. True Jehovah worship is exclusive and certainly is boring compared to that séance. I know that the apparition pretending to be my brother was not really Thomas. Someone or something was deliberately trying to deceive me. Josie, I do see a real change in Debra. She is so happy and self-confident now, but Zalith has always been that way. Naamah says any doubts should be gone after we personally witnessed the Flood as God's judgment on a violent world. Zalith doesn't believe Jehovah sent the Flood, He just claims that He did. Zalith claims that maybe it is a normal cleansing cycle of the earth, like the waves on the shore. She said maybe the earth just knows when it needs to be cleansed; such floods probably have happened every few thousand years for eons. How do I know that isn't true? And maybe the Flood didn't cover and destroy the whole earth. Maybe it was just our part of the world that was destroyed. Naamah tells us that the earth is only 1657 years old, specifically created by God, while Zalith claims it has always existed."

Just then Noah entered the aviary. Cassie hoped he hadn't heard any of her theological discussion with Josie. Although she wasn't entirely sure that Zalith was right, she didn't want to betray her friend.

"Cassia, I really do want to thank you for taking such good care of the birds. It is always so clean and pleasant in here."

"Thank you Father Noah, but I enjoy it. I think the birds are my favorites," she said as she placed Josie back in her cage.

Noah lifted Josie from her perch and held her securely but gently, between his left elbow and chest with his right hand on her back and started to leave.

Cassie began to panic, "Father Noah where are you taking her?"

"I am going to release her to see if the earth is ready for us."

"But what if she doesn't return, like the raven?"

"Then we will have our answer, she has found dry land. Cassie, I am sure the raven is fine, we can see mountaintops near enough for him to find food and shelter. But doves require trees and branches in which to nest. If the dove comes back, that will tell me she prefers the Ark over whatever conditions she finds outside of it."

All day long Cassie worried. She didn't eat, she couldn't pay attention during her lessons, and she wasn't even sure she did her chores correctly. She couldn't keep her mind off Josie. Finally at evening time, she heard a familiar coo. She rushed outside just in time to see Josie flying to Noah and perching on his finger.

"Thank goodness she has returned safely! I'll take her Father Noah."

Even though all the animals do seem to trust him, he doesn't seem to care for their precious lives very much, Cassie resentfully thought as she took Josie back to her cage.

Chapter 39
The Ark, 2348 BC

It was long past midnight when Shem and Debra finished drying off the new triplets that Blackie, Debra's favorite ewe, had just delivered. When they made sure that all three had nursed and Blackie was doing well, they put down clean straw and went to bed.

***

Zalith was beginning to feel that she would never be able to make a proper sacrifice to her goddess. With Debra having a bodyguard and strict orders that Zalith herself was never to be left alone, a human sacrifice was no longer an option, at least for now. *None of the others were expendable, anyway.* She slipped out of bed being careful not to wake Ham and went to search the animal quarters for something small enough for her to handle, but that would be perfect enough to please Inanna.

What luck. Inanna has provided her own sacrifice. Three newborn lambs, probably no one even knows they were born yet; their umbilical cords are still wet. Noah and the others will be happy enough with twins. They are still so young and innocent, a proper sacrifice indeed.

She reached over and grabbed the lamb closest to the rail, thankful she didn't need to actually enter the pen. Of course the lamb began to bleat, so that Zalith had to immediately strangle it with the cotton cord she brought with her, just for such a purpose.

She prayed over the lamb, offering it to Inanna. The ceremony was shorter than normal, Zalith didn't want to risk discovery. She wished that she could burn it: not only was that the custom of the Temple sacrifice, but also burning would have destroyed the remains. *Now what? The ground outside is too dry to throw the lamb's body overboard, it could be seen from the deck. Of course! I'll feed it to one of the animals.* She quickly carried it to the carnivore corridor, hurriedly threw it into the first pen, the cats, and ran back to her room. *I do hate those cats; the only thing they are good for is fur,* as she thought about her cape lined with the fur of the white tiger – the one she was wearing the day that Cassie saw her kill the buck. *Poor dumb Cassie! She puts so much emphasis on animal life, when will she learn? Sometimes lying is the best choice when dealing with Cassie, like when she discovered that beautiful cape in my wardrobe. Luckily, she readily believed me when I told her the tiger had died of natural causes. She believes everything I tell her, a perfect assistant, but she does have those qualms about killing animals; I won't even mention the word sacrifice to her, not for a long time.*

***

Debra and Shem hurried to the sheep pens to check on the newborns before breakfast. Debra looked at Shem and asked, "There were three last night. I didn't imagine triplets, did I?

Shem was just as confused. "Yes, Blackie delivered triplets, but where is the third? I suppose it wouldn't be that unusual for one of them not to survive, but where is the body?"

They looked at each other and simultaneously said, "Zalith!"

"I don't know how or why, but I am sure she had something to do with this," Shem said empathically.

Japheth appeared, "I found some pieces of wool and 4 tiny little cloven feet in the cat pen. Are we missing a lamb?"

"Yes, Jay" Shem continued, "Last night Blackie delivered triplets, and now there are only twins. I guess that explains it. But how did it get there? The pens are secure; there is no way it could have escaped. The gate was closed when we arrived this morning and I know that I closed it last night as well. A newborn wouldn't wander that far away from its mother. If the cat were loose, it could jump in here with the sheep, but the other way around? Its all very strange."

Everything that Shem said made sense to Debra. No one would wake up in the middle of the night and feed Blackie's baby to the cats. However, she was sure it wasn't a bazaar accident.

Zalith made a sacrifice to Inanna and then disposed of the body by feeding it to the cats. But I'm sure no one will believe me! They'll think I'm having a relapse and start counting the wine casks.

"I think it is a sign that we need to get everybody and everything off this boat, there could be mass carnage down here soon," Jay said as he walked away.

"Let's not mention this to the others. My Dad has enough to worry about and we can't prove that it was Zalith" Shem told Debra on the way to the breakfast table.

164

Chapter 40

The Ark 2348 BC

"Shem, how many days have we been here?" Noah asked at breakfast.

"Seems like about a million, but this is the 278th day, according to my records."

"I'm going to send the dove out again today to test the outside conditions."

"Father Noah, send me," volunteered Cassie, worried about the safety of her pet. "I can certainly be a better spy than the dove,"

Noah laughed, not realizing that Cassie was entirely serious.

Japheth firmly took her hand, "Cassie, don't be ridiculous. I am not going to risk any harm coming to you, or our unborn child."

Cassie was consumed with worry all day, but was relieved when Josie again returned in the evening, this time with an olive branch in her mouth.

At dinner, everyone was elated. "When are we leaving the Ark, Dad?" Ham asked excitedly, "The bird brought back a green branch!"

"We will wait another week, and release her again. It's when she doesn't come back that we will know the earth is ready for us. We will also soon remove part of the roof, to let in fresh air and to give us wood to build pens and houses."

Cassie ran crying to her room. No one was surprised, believing her pregnancy was making her over-emotional about finally disembarking. Zalith was secretly pleased; she knew that every one of Noah's actions of which Cassie disapproved would only broaden the gap between Cassie and the Jehovah worshippers and bring Cassie closer to her own beliefs.

***

The next week seemed to last forever, except to Cassie. Not only was she fearful of Josie's demise, but also she knew the passing of every day was bringing them closer to the end of their adventure on the Ark. She still was apprehensive about being the wife and mother; the one who runs the household and whom everyone depends upon. She didn't feel capable. She hoped they would be living with Naamah and Noah. *What am I going to do without servants?*

This time, Josie didn't return in the evening. Everyone except Cassia was expectantly happy. She didn't come to dinner that night. When Japheth returned to see if she needed anything, he told her that his Dad was going to keep them on the Ark for yet another month. He smiled as he vowed to never set foot on a boat again. When he left, Cassie tried to sleep, but could only worry about burned dinners, crying children, and dirty laundry.

Chapter 41
The Ark, 2348 BC

"Didn't you think the purification ceremony went well, Naamah?"

"Yes, Noah, extremely well. But how could they have had any doubts, after going through the past year. God told you to build the Ark, in order to save you, your family, and the animals. You did, the Flood came, and we all survived. I don't see why God's sovereignty would have ever been questioned."

"I don't know either, but remember the dream? The Liar can attack in very subtle ways. If he appeared as something recognizable, no one would be tempted. It's when he appears as something beautiful and apparently harmless that we are tricked by his lies. I just wanted to make sure the girls have a solid background and a public commitment to help them ward off his attacks. I feel responsible; I should have personally made sure of their spiritual salvation long ago. None of them were raised with a godly influence, you know."

"They all seemed so willing, especially Zalith."

"I suppose that time will tell, her confession and repentance seemed real enough." Noah still had some doubts about Zalith's authenticity. *Why do I feel so uneasy in her presence? Maybe its just because she is so pretty. Maybe.*

"How are the preparations for tomorrow's departure going? Did the girls get all the food stores and the kitchen utensils packed?"

"Yes, we are ready. Things to leave immediately are packed; others are to stay here. Didn't you say we would eat and sleep on the Ark for yet a little while?"

"I think that will be easier. I know the boys and their wives will be disappointed, but there is no sense in stressing to build pens, barns and houses all in one day."

Noah turned and absentmindedly pulled on his beard "Naamah, it's strange, but the animals are suddenly very anxious and jumpy, especially those from the forest. We have cared for them for over a year now and they were very calm and responsive, but this morning they shied away from us and some were visibly trembling in our presence."

"That is strange, but I am sure God is in control of their actions. They wouldn't all have the same sudden strange behavior if there weren't some outside influence."

"Yes, Naamah, you must be right. It would be unrealistic to live in peace with wild lions, bears, and those giant lizards. They don't reason as we do. We would be defenseless if they decided to have us for lunch. It *is* a good thing they have become afraid of us. You are so insightful!"

Chapter 42

The Ark, Thursday, December 18, 2348 BC

Nobody slept very well. They were all up before dawn; anxiously awaiting the word from Noah that it was time to leave. Zalith had packed her idol, spell books, potions, crystal ball and special candles neatly hidden in her trunks, wrapped in her sumptuous silks. She wasn't sure how she was going to keep them hidden, but she had faith that they were important enough that her goddess would aid her. She had another secret that she realized she couldn't hide very long, especially from Ham. She, like Cassia was pregnant. Her spirit guides had not yet told her if she should continue the pregnancy or not.

***

Cassie was upset that many of her special pets seemed to not even recognize her, but she really didn't have the time to worry about it now. She hastily packed the rest of their belongings and sat on the bed waiting for Jay.

When he arrived, she blurted out, "Where are we going to sleep tonight? You won't be able to build us a house in one day."

"As much as I don't want to, we might have to use the Ark for shelter for awhile. Dad will decide. I think he brought some large tents. Don't worry, I'll take care of you." He kissed her on the head and went back to help his brothers with the preparations for leaving.

Cassie was bored; no one would let her do any heavy lifting and she was done with her assigned work, so she went to see Zalith. Just as she expected, Zalith was also in her room, letting the others attend to the work.

"Cassie, come in, come in. Guess what! My mother's spirit was here again this morning. She was very reassuring that things will be all right. Sit down, and let me tell you what she said."

Cassie found a place to sit on the one chair that wasn't stacked with bags and wooden boxes.

"So what did your mother have to say?" she asked as she awkwardly crossed her knees. "This baby is getting in my way, I can't wait for him to be born."

Zalith laughed. "That's when the work starts, you will wish you were pregnant again. Anyway, my mother told me not to worry about having to be secretive, it will seem like a long time, but eventually things will be able to be out in the open. She said to think of our hiding as a transformation, like a butterfly. The butterfly hides in the cocoon, in the darkness and then emerges with its true identity: beautiful and brightly colored, the envy of all who see her."

"Zalith, that's such a beautiful picture. Do you think the butterfly is the symbol that the vision told us about at the séance?"

"Perhaps, at least it is a symbol of our waiting. Every time we see a butterfly, real or artistic, we are to remember our glorious unfolding that is waiting for just the right moment. While we are waiting, we have to be vigilant. The spirit world will send us coded signals and we will need to recognize them. Some will be ones only I can understand, maybe some that you will understand, but the others will just be blinded by their belief in Jehovah. Maybe there is something more beautiful coming. I just have a feeling that the spirits are trying to tell me something. But look at what I am making. "

Zalith pulled one of her skirts from her sewing bag and showed Cassie the half-embroidered butterfly on the soft and luxurious mauve-colored material.

"That's so pretty!" Cassie exclaimed, "I'd rather have it adorning my wall or maybe a pillow instead of wearing it, but that will look stunning on you."

"Oh, I almost forgot. My Mother said that you would deliver a girl, a special child, one that we will raise in the faith and who will become a great priestess. We will have to be very secretive about it, at least at first. You should feel grateful to be so selected."

Ham rushed in. "Hurry you two, the great door is open, and we are almost ready to make the first trip out. Dad wants us all to pray together first so lets go and get that over with. Jay is looking for you, Cassie."

Cassie was glad for the interruption and the excuse to leave. She didn't know how to reply to the prophesy about her child.

***

Zalith smiled to herself, *Mother said it is my child that will fulfill the prophecy, but it doesn't hurt to make Cassie feel important and part of the divine plan. Now I can tell Ham and the others that I am pregnant.*

"Ham wait. I want to tell you something first. We are going to have a baby."

"Zalith!" Ham, elated, picked her up and held her close. Although he was happy about this news, he momentarily wished that she had chosen a less hurried and busy time to tell him so that they could have savored the moment together.

"Lets go tell the others. I don't want you carrying anything or standing too long, either."

Zalith again smiled to herself as Ham excitedly led her to the others, waiting for departure. *Finally, a pregnancy I don't have to hide. I don't have to distance myself from the growing child; I can nurture and love it. We will be close, as I was to my mother. I can and will enjoy this pregnancy, with everyone, especially Ham, waiting on me. The mother of the future high priestess should rightfully be pampered.*

***

Cassie found Japheth in their room. She immediately demanded some answers.

"Jay, your Dad and brothers aren't just going to let all the animals loose at once are they? The little ones will be trampled in the stampede or even devoured."

"Cassie, haven't you learned by now that my Dad thinks of everything? He has a plan. The smaller animals will be carried out in their cages and turned loose in the brush. Now that the water and dry land are separated again, we will need to transport the coast dwellers like the seals to water by horse-drawn carts. We have to build pens before we bring the farm animals out…"

"I'm sorry, Jay. It's just that sometimes I think that I am the only one that can take care of them."

"Let's go. My parents are waiting for us."

The Rainbow's Dark Shadow

Chapter 43

Mt. Ararat, December 18, 2348 BC

They couldn't contain their excitement for one more moment. Even Naamah, the icon of patience, was beginning to become impatient. "Noah, what are we waiting for?" she asked.

"I just don't want to make any empty trips. We should all carry something. Lets take the insect farms first, and the other smaller animals."

"Ham, I am not carrying rats or mice, and especially not any crawly or creepy things." Zalith whispered to her husband.

"Dad, Zalith is pregnant, I don't want her to do anything that might upset or hurt her. You know that she can't stand mice and squiggly things."

. Now seems like a strange time to announce her pregnancy, Noah thought as Naamah and Cassie began to congratulate and hug her. *Just when we were starting to get organized and actually leave, the focus is shifted to Zalith and her needs. Cassie isn't complaining.*

"Zalith, you can carry one of the butterfly cages, they are pretty and the cage is lightweight," Noah said to her, hiding his annoyance.

"I want to pray and we can jointly thank God for saving us. Every one come over and join hands."

***

The last thing Shem wanted to do was hold Zalith's hand. Debra quickly situated herself between Naamah and Shem. When Zalith took his other hand he was forced to hold hers or make a scene. *I can't move, then Debra would be next to her. I'll just have to....why is her hand so hot? It's like holding a hot piece of iron. Just hurry up, Dad. I can't think of anything but Zalith and I am sure that is her intention. She is a witch!*

***

Zalith bowed her head so that no one saw her secret smile. She had long ago learned to concentrate her inner energy to make her hands hot to the touch. She knew the burning hand trick was upsetting Shem and that there was nothing he could do. *I won't let him ignore me!*

***

Noah made the prayer short, every one, including himself, was getting anxious to set foot on dry land. He knew that a longer and more formal thanksgiving would be held at the planned sacrifices, the seventh clean animal and bird was brought for that purpose.

"We have a lot to accomplish today, so lets get going!"

Noah and Naamah led the family procession down the door turned gangplank. Every one was laughing and joyful. Cassie and Japheth took off their shoes and let the cool new grass caress their feet for the first time in over a year.

As they were releasing some of the rabbits, Naamah asked Noah, "isn't it remarkable how God provides? I know that in Eden the animals did not eat each other, but now that they do, it is so amazing how God makes sure for all of their various provisions. The rats, mice, rabbits and other small animals reproduce so much faster than the larger predatory animals; if they didn't, both prey and hunter would perish off the face of the earth."

"Yes God provides, but He also made us responsible for their care. We will need to place the rest of the dried fish and meat strategically out for the meat-eaters for a little while yet. There is plenty of grass so that we can reserve the grain and hay stores for the farm animals. The first thing that the boys and I need to do is make some pens for them. We don't need them to wander off and get lost, or devoured their first few days in the new world. Did you notice that roughly half of the dogs ran off and the other half stayed with us, watchfully lounging by the farm animals as if the dogs wanted to protect them? I had noticed yesterday that some of the dogs were suddenly hiding in the back of their pens, and snarling in fear. I suppose God wants there to be both wild and domestic dogs. I know He has His reasons, but I would just as soon have all the dogs on our side, wouldn't you?"

Naamah laughed, " Do you think God would bring us this far to let us be eaten by wild dogs?"

Noah sighed, "No. I am just thinking about the differences in how the animals respond to us now, and it seems sad; but we have other things to worry about. We will have to sleep and eat on the Ark until we can build houses, and I am not sure that this is the area in which God wants us to settle. We may just pitch the tents for a little while. I am sure He will tell me soon. If we stay in this area we can use the lumber from the Ark, but if we are to move further, it's just too much to carry."

Noah began to gather stones and stack them in a rectangular structure, as the other men labored to build pens for the farm animals and then relocate them

"Boys, you will need to make a covering for the poultry pens by interlacing some of the bamboo slats that we used for bird cages." Noah said as he continued to build the altar.

***

"Jay what is your Dad doing?" Cassie asked.

Japheth glanced in his father's direction. "He's building an altar to sacrifice to Jehovah."

"Sacrifice? No! Jay he can't!" Cassie started to run over to try to stop Noah from what she perceived as a cruel and unnecessary ceremony. Jay gently grabbed her arm and pulled her close to him.

"Cassie, I don't understand it either, but we just have to accept it. We have to trust my father."

"But how many animals? Just one, I hope." Cassie began to cry, wondering which one would be lost. Whether their soul was released to a better place as Zalith said or not, *she* would never see them again. For the first time she was glad that Josie had been released earlier to escape such a fate.

"Jay, if God is a spirit, why does he need to be fed?" Cassie asked through angry tears.

"My parents tell me the sacrifices are not to feed God. It is the giving up of something valuable to honor God, to demonstrate that He is more important than anything we own. Like I said, I don't totally understand either, but in addition to giving up something, the animals somehow take our place. They suffer for our wrongdoing. It is also to show thankfulness for God saving us. He could have destroyed us along with everything else."

"Jay, it just isn't fair!" Cassie buried her head in his chest and pulled his shirt over her ears to try to close out the bleating sounds and shield her nose from the aroma of the burning sacrifices. She had made her decision. *I will never bow to such a cruel god. Neither will my children.*

***

Cassie smiled, relieving some of Jay's anxiety He didn't realize her relaxation and smile were the result of a monumental spiritual decision.

Jay knew they had brought one extra of each clean animal and bird, to provide the animals needed for the sacrificial ritual, but he didn't want to upset Cassie anymore. He was hoping his father wasn't going to make all the sacrifices today. *How can I choose between Cassie and my parents? I hope it never comes to that.*

***

Noah continued with the sacrifices, discarding the skin, bones and entrails and placing the rest of the animal on the stone altar. When he finished placing the last animal, a bullock, on the hot stones and put more wood on the fire, he joined Naamah already on her knees deep in prayer. Shem and Debra were near, holding hands and also on their knees. Ham and Zalith were behind them, heads bowed but still standing. Japheth and Cassia were standing even further back; Cassie's back was to the altar, her body shaking with sobs.

Suddenly colorful light flooded the scene, as the Rainbow appeared for the first time. Ham felt Zalith's hand fall from his. He turned. *Was she OK? Had she fainted?* Zalith was on the ground, head bowed. The colors of the rainbow made streaks on her hair and back. Tears were brimming up in his eyes; it was so beautiful! She was so beautiful. Her reverence touched Ham deeply, and he bent down to pray beside his beloved wife. *Her conversion was real. I will try to be more like her, I will God, I promise.*

***

Zalith was so deep in prayer, thanking Inanna and pledging eternal bondage to her that she didn't notice Ham's tender reaction, nor feel his hand gently squeezing hers.

***

"Cassie, Look! Turn around!" Jay joyfully told her.

Cassie turned, and she too fell on her knees. Jay also bowed down, wanting to help and support his pregnant wife. *This has to be from Inanna: awesome and beautiful, so very beautiful. How gentle and what a contrast to the horrid sacrifices! Noah will no doubt claim the colorful arc is from his Jehovah, but that was exactly what Inanna had said he would do.*

They simultaneously looked up as a voice declared from heaven:

WHILE THE EARTH REMAINETH, SEEDTIME AND HARVEST, AND COLD AND HEAT, AND SUMMER AND WINTER, AND DAY AND NIGHT SHALL NOT CEASE.

BE FRUITFUL AND MULTIPLY, AND REPLENISH THE EARTH AND THE FEAR OF YOU AND THE DREAD OF YOU SHALL BE UPON EVERY BEAST OF THE EARTH, AND UPON EVERY FOWL OF THE AIR, UPON ALL THAT MOVETH UPON THE EARTH, AND UPON THE FISHES OF THE SEA; INTO YOUR HAND ARE THEY DELIVERED

EVERY MOVING THING THAT LIVETH SHALL BE MEAT FOR YOU; EVEN AS THE GREEN HERB HAVE I GIVEN YOU ALL THINGS.

BUT FLESH WITH THE LIFE THEREOF, WHICH IS THE BLOOD THEREOF, SHALL YE NOT EAT.

AND SURELY YOUR BLOOD OF LIVES WILL I REQUIRE: AT THE HAND OF EVERY BEAST WILL I REQUIRE IT, AND AT THE HAND OF MAN; AT THE HAND OF EVERY MAN'S BROTHER WILL I REQUIRE THE LIFE OF A MAN.

WHOSO SHEDDETH MAN'S BLOOD, BY MAN SHALL HIS BLOOD BE SHED: FOR IN THE IMAGE OF GOD MADE HE MAN

AND YOU, BE YE FRUITFUL AND MULTIPLY: BRING FORTH ABUNDANTLY IN THE EARTH, AND MULTIPLY THEREIN

AND I, BEHOLD, I ESTABLISH MY COVENANT WITH YOU, AND WITH YOUR SEED AFTER YOU;

AND WITH EVERY LIVING CREATURE THAT IS WITH YOU, OF THE FOWL OF THE CATTLE, AND OF EVERY BEAST OF THE EARTH WITH YOU; FROM ALL THAT GO OUT OF THE ARK, TO EVERY BEAST OF THE EARTH.

AND I WILL ESTABLISH MY COVENANT WITH YOU: NEITHER WILL ALL FLESH BE CUT OFF ANY MORE FROM THE WATERS OF A FLOOD; NEITHER SHALL THERE BE A FLOOD TO DESTROY THE EARTH.

THIS IS THE TOKEN OF THE COVENANT WHICH I MAKE BETWEEN ME AND YOU, AND EVERY LIVING CREATURE THAT IS WITH YOU, FOR PERPETUAL GENERATIONS

I DO SET MY BOW IN THE CLOUD, AND IT SHALL BE A TOKEN OF A COVENANT BETWEEN ME AND THE EARTH

To be continued in Volume II:

About the Author

Dr. Sharon Cargo practices veterinary medicine in Southern California. She earned a Bachelors of Science in Nutrition from the College of Agriculture of the Ohio State University, a Doctorate of Veterinary Medicine from the Ohio State University and a Masters of Science Education from The Institute for Creation Research. Her unique background of animal husbandry and creation science blends naturally into the study of Noah's Ark. She and her husband, Bob, have three children and one grandchild.